"I only came he
maybe be a part o

"And," he continued, back to Denver with m

He could almost see Arabella's stomach clench and knot.

"Can we go somewhere and talk?" he asked.

Jonathan waited a couple of heartbeats, wondering if Arabella Michaels would show him some sympathy and listen to him. Arabella *Clayton* Michaels, he reminded himself. From what he'd heard, the Clayton name sure carried a lot of weight around here. And there always seemed to be several Claytons around at any given time.

She bit at her wide, pouty lip. Jonathan watched her, fascinated with the stubborn slant of her chin and the glint of dare in her catlike gold-brown eyes. When she focused those big eyes on him, he couldn't take his next breath.

This woman stood between him and his niece.

* * *

LENORA WORTH

has written and contracted over 50 books. Her career with Love Inspired Books spans fourteen years. Her very first Love Inspired title, *The Wedding Quilt,* won *Affaire de Coeur*'s Best Inspirational for 1997, and *Logan's Child* won an *RT Book Reviews* Best Love Inspired for 1998. Her Love Inspired Suspense *Body of Evidence* became a *New York Times* bestseller. With millions of books in print, Lenora continues to write for the Love Inspired and Love Inspired Suspense lines and Harlequin's Superromance. Lenora also wrote a weekly opinion column for the local paper and worked freelance with a local magazine. She writes fiction full-time now and is enjoying adventures with her retired husband, Don. Married for thirty-six years, they have two grown children. Lenora enjoys writing, reading and shopping… especially shoe shopping.

The Doctor's Family
Lenora Worth

Love Inspired

Special thanks and acknowledgment to Lenora Worth for her participation in the Rocky Mountain Heirs miniseries

PLEASE RECYCLE
THIS PRODUCT IS RECYCLABLE

Recycling programs
for this product may
not exist in your area.

LOVE INSPIRED BOOKS

ISBN-13: 978-0-373-81570-8

THE DOCTOR'S FAMILY

Copyright © 2011 by Harlequin Books S.A.

www.LoveInspiredBooks.com

Printed in U.S.A.

And I will be a father to you, and you shall be sons
and daughters to Me, says the Lord Almighty.
—*2 Corinthians* 6:18

To all of my wonderful editors:

Patience Bloom, Emily Rodmell, Tina James
and Melissa Endlich.

Thanks to each of you for allowing me
to use my imagination and create my stories.

Chapter One

This was probably a bad idea.

Arabella Clayton Michaels headed toward the back door of the big industrial kitchen inside the Clayton Christian Church fellowship hall. The Wednesday-night meeting of the Church Care Committee was about to get started, but she was determined to check the parking lot for a silver sports car. She had a sneaking suspicion that she'd find that stranger hovering outside, the same stranger who seemed to be following her around town.

"Hey, Arabella, Zach's looking for you."

Arabella turned to where Gabe Wesson stood with some other men who'd helped set up the tables and chairs and were now waiting for the meal to commence. "Thanks. I'll be right back. I have to take care of something."

She didn't wait for a response, nor did she look for her cousin Zach. She'd talk to him later, after she found Mr. City Slicker and set him straight.

Her crinkled denim skirt flew out over her worn red cowboy boots as she took the back steps, her arms wrapped against the soft chenille of the blue sweater she wore over a white button-up shirt. The fall temperature cooled with each dip of the golden sunset over the Rocky Mountains to the west.

But the chill covering Arabella didn't come from the crisp fall air. It came from a fear deep inside her heart. A fear that refused to let go. Arabella had an awful feeling her routine life was about to change. She couldn't explain this feeling but it was there, holding her down with all the heaviness of an anvil.

She'd felt this way since the day her grandfather, George Clayton, Sr., had passed away. Arabella was the only grandchild who'd stayed here in the tiny Colorado town of Clayton, founded and named after her ancestors. The feeling of a change coming in the wind had increased after the reading of her grandpa's will. The ornery old man had left $250,000 plus five hundred acres of Clayton real estate to each of his six grandchildren—with certain stipulations, of course. One of them being that the other five adult grandchildren had to return to Clayton and live here for a year—or no one got their inheritance.

And Arabella, a single mother with triplet girls, would be forced out of the old Victorian home known as Clayton House. If her uncle Samuel's family had its way, she'd already have been booted out without a second glance. The other side of the

Clayton family had hard feelings about the will. Because her grandfather had stipulated that if her cousins didn't come home to honor his request everything would revert to his brother Samuel, Arabella figured any slipup on her part could be used as fodder for Uncle Samuel's case.

That was why she was so concerned about this stranger lurking around town. What if her uncle had hired this man to spy on her and her cousins?

She intended to confront the man and ask him outright what he was doing here. Jasmine, the teenage girl who'd lived with Arabella for the past three years, had seen the stranger's sleek silver car earlier near the park.

The newcomer was probably a private detective hired by Samuel Clayton because he stood to inherit everything if her cousins didn't cooperate and come home. Or just as bad, the man could have been sent by her ex-husband, Harry. It'd be just like Harry to hear about her possible inheritance and try to muscle in on things, even if the man did send sporadic checks to help with his daughters' care and well-being.

She'd fight this, not because of the money, even though money would be nice. She had to fight for her three little girls. And the first thing she'd tell the stranger she'd seen hanging around last month and again today—take a long hike up a tall mountain.

She came around the back of the white clapboard

church and squinted into the golden threads of the sunset. And saw the glint of a silver car flashing on the edge of the lot near a cluster of aspen trees.

Hurrying, her boots clomping on the pavement, Arabella didn't stop to think. With both hands she tried to open the car's passenger-side door then looked through the dark windows.

The car was empty.

Then she heard a male voice behind her.

"Looking for me?"

Arabella whirled to face the man who had caused her nightmares over the past few days. "You could say that. I don't like the way you've been watching me and my family. I want it to stop." She glared at him. "Just so you know, my cousin is the deputy sheriff. I've already alerted him about you. He's probably doing a background check as we speak."

Her cousin Zach had told her not to confront the man on her own. Too late for that now.

The man stepped forward, his dark blond hair as rich and golden as the glistening dusk. He looked good in his nice-fitting jeans, fancy boots and wool sports coat. But even the worst of criminals could dress with movie-star quality.

"You've got it all wrong," he said, holding up one hand, a whiff of something spicy and woodsy drifting around him. "I can explain—"

"You'd better start talking, then," Arabella said,

her hands on her hips. "Beginning with why you've been lurking around my girls and me. I saw you a few weeks back and now here you are again. What do you want?"

He stepped closer, his smoky blue-gray eyes sparkling with interest and intent. "I have a good reason for…following you."

"Yeah, and I think I know what it is."

"No, honestly, it's nothing sinister or criminal. It's a bit complicated. I'm Jonathan, Jonathan Turner."

Arabella deciphered that and the bold look in his eyes. "Turner? That's Jasmine's last name."

"I know," he said, letting out a soft breath. "Her father, Aaron, was my older brother. I'm Jasmine's uncle."

Arabella grabbed onto the sports car, her breath hitching in her throat. "What?"

She heard the church door banging shut, then Zach calling out her name. But she couldn't move, couldn't take her eyes off this man. Up close he looked like a younger, better version of Jasmine's father, Aaron Turner. She'd only seen Aaron a couple of times around town, but the resemblance was right there, staring her in the eyes.

Taking a quick breath, she asked, "What did you say?"

He stood in front of her now. "I'm telling you the

truth, Mrs. Michaels. I'm Jasmine's uncle. I've been trying to locate her…and last month I asked around to make sure I had the right girl. And now I know I do."

"I don't believe you." Or maybe she just didn't *want* to believe him. Arabella didn't like change and lately change had been coming her way with all the haste of the falling leaves around her.

Zach walked up, scowled his deputy sheriff's frown at the man standing there and then took Arabella by the arm. "It's true, Arabella. I tried to find you to tell you. I ran a background check on him this afternoon. He's telling you the truth. Jonathan Turner is Jasmine's uncle."

Then Zach turned to Jonathan. "And all that aside, you'd better have a very good reason for messing with my cousin and her family, Dr. Turner."

Arabella looked from Zach to the man he just addressed as Dr. Turner. "A doctor? I can't believe this. We imagined all kinds of horrid things. When we first saw you, we thought you reminded us of someone, but I never dreamed—" She stopped, her hands fisting at her sides. "That was mighty mean, what you did to us. What you did to that girl, sneaking around like that."

Jonathan lowered his head, forcing her to look at him. "I'm not trying to frighten you. Honestly. I only came here to find my niece…and maybe be a part of her life. I live in Denver and I thought

Jasmine should at least know me." He took a deep breath before continuing. "And, to be frank, I wouldn't mind if she came back to Denver with me."

Arabella's stomach knotted. So this was it, then—that something terrible she'd been dreading. This man had come here to rearrange her carefully constructed life.

Or so he thought.

"Can we go somewhere and talk?"

Jonathan waited a couple of heartbeats, wondering if he'd be arrested for harassment or if Arabella Michaels would show him some sympathy and listen to him. Arabella *Clayton* Michaels, he reminded himself. From what he'd heard, the Clayton name sure carried a lot of weight around here. And there always seemed to be several Claytons around at any given time.

She bit at her wide, pouty lip then glanced over at the uniformed deputy sheriff—what was his name…Zach? Jonathan watched her, fascinated with the stubborn slant of her chin and the glint of dare in her catlike gold-brown eyes. When she tossed back piles of silky brown hair then focused those big eyes on him, he couldn't take his next breath. He waited for her decision, thinking that must be the reason he couldn't think straight. This woman stood between him and his niece.

She cut her gaze toward the sheriff. "Zach, thank you for the update. Could you excuse us, please?"

Zach held up a hand. "Arabella, I don't think—"

"I've got this, Zach. Just…keep Jasmine occupied until I can figure out what to do."

"Is she inside?" Jonathan asked, hoping to meet his niece at last.

"She is, but you don't need to bother her right now." The woman turned to her cousin. "Zach, please?"

Zach didn't look convinced. He pivoted toward Jonathan, his brow furrowing. "I don't know what kind of game you're running here, but if you do anything to hurt Arabella or her family, you'll have me to deal with. Understand?"

Although Jonathan respected the man for doing his job and trying to protect his cousin, he'd been more intimidated by gang members brought into the E.R. with gunshot wounds. "I read you. I only want to get to know my niece."

Zach dropped his hand. "I'll be inside if you need me, Arabella."

She nodded, then waited for Zach to stalk away.

"Protective, isn't he?" Jonathan said by way of getting through the icy chill in her eyes.

She gave him a look that could crumble Pike's Peak. "Claytons stand together. Well, at least my side of the family does anyway."

Hmm. Trouble in Claytonville? Jonathan filed

that away for another time. Right now he wanted to discuss why he was here. "I admire that. And I'm sorry I scared you."

He motioned to a bench inside the spot marked as a prayer garden. Tall trees and fat shrubs gave the walled-off area a sense of seclusion. Inside, a fountain bubbled in the center, and colorful, fat mums bloomed in shades of red, orange and yellow in the flower beds. A plaque showing praying hands read "He will not leave you comfortless." Maybe the serenity of the place would calm both of them down.

She followed him, then sank against the stone bench, putting her elbows on her knees and leaning over, her head in her hands. "I thought you were some sort of private investigator or, worse, a creep."

He had to smile at that. "I'm neither, although I've been called worse. Lots of times."

She sat up straight, adjusting her shoulders into what looked like fight mode. "I can't imagine why. You sneak around spying on people. I'm a mother with small children. Why didn't you just come to my front door and tell me the truth?"

He didn't have a good answer for that. Shrugging, he said, "I'm not good at confrontations."

She shot him a measuring look. "You're a doctor?"

"Yeah. I'm better at telling people what I can and can't fix. Not so good in the emotional part of the conversations."

"So your bedside manner is lacking as much as your social skills?"

He grinned, glad she had a sense of humor. "Somewhat, or so I've been told."

Her lips pursed at that comment. "And you live in Denver?"

"Denver, yes. I have a high-rise condo near the hospital."

She stared out at the aspen trees lining the parking lot. "Not so far away."

"No, not really. An hour or so."

"You can't take Jasmine away." She took in a breath, then stared over at him.

"Excuse me? She's not a kid. I don't plan on *taking* her away. But I am going to offer her a place to live if she wants it. I owe her that at least."

She gave him another glaring look, but her expression softened. "You heard me. You can't just barge in here and expect Jasmine to clap her hands in glee and pack her bags. She's eighteen now and making her own decisions. And besides, this is her home. She was born here."

"And had a bad life here from what I've heard."

Arabella leveled him with a scathing glance. "Yes, and where were you when she was having that horrible life? Where were you when she lived in that filthy apartment for months and months after Aaron Turner up and left?"

He had to swallow the lump of regret in his throat. "I didn't know—"

"You didn't know or you didn't care? Were you so busy doctoring you couldn't even check on your own family?"

"My brother and I…were estranged. We hadn't spoken in years. I didn't know where he was."

"And you apparently didn't try to find out."

"Yes, I did," Jonathan said, getting up to pace across the brick tiles. "I did. Many times. But Aaron wasn't one for sending greeting cards. He could hold a grudge, that's for sure."

"And where is he now? Or do you even care?"

A sick feeling hit Jonathan in his stomach. "You mean, you haven't heard? He's dead. He died about a month ago in a car crash. He was driving drunk."

Arabella put a knuckle to her mouth. "Oh, no. Oh, my goodness. Jasmine doesn't know that. No one contacted us." She gripped the bench, her hands down beside her skirt. "How am I supposed to tell her that?"

Jonathan wished he could make it easier. "She has to hear it—and understand I just found out a few weeks ago. I'd have come sooner if I'd known. I didn't even get to attend his funeral."

"And why didn't you know? Why didn't you two keep up with each other?"

Jonathan looked down at the pretty garden tiles. "He hated me. Because I left. I got out."

"Got out?"

Jonathan wasn't ready to give her an up-close-and-personal history of his family dysfunctions. "It doesn't matter. We drifted apart after…after our daddy died. But I'm here now. I don't want to let the same thing happen with Jasmine. I want her to know she has an uncle."

"And how will your family feel about this?"

He glanced at the praying hands set in stone. "I don't have a family. I'm not married and our mother died when we were little. Our father died years later."

"That's tough—losing your mother like that. I'm sorry."

He nodded at the understanding in her eyes. "That's why I want to get to know Jasmine. I'm her only close relative."

She stood, too, anger seeming to push away her compassion. "And you're willing to entice her to the big city even though she doesn't know you? Have you even considered what that might do to her?"

"More than you can imagine," he said, his own doubts matching the darkness in her eyes. "As you said, she's an adult now. Neither of us can force her to do anything. I hear she's engaged to some kid— Cade Clayton. Are you related to him?"

"He's a cousin, yes. Second cousin. His daddy, Charley, is my cousin. And let me tell you, you don't want to mess with Charley Clayton or his two stubborn brothers." She sighed. "He's fighting this marriage and he'll fight you, too, if you start in on Cade."

Jonathan pressed two fingers against the throbbing in his forehead. "I'm getting that we have some good Claytons and some not-so-good around here. Am I right?"

"Unfortunately, yes. Our uncle Samuel has three sons—Charley, Pauley—our honorable mayor—and Frank. He's the quiet one who lives on the outskirts of town. But between them and their offspring, it's always high drama around here." She glanced toward the church. "Listen, I need to get back inside. I'll have to make up an excuse if Jasmine sees you. We can't blurt this out in front of everyone inside."

Jonathan wasn't ready to let her go. "Wait. This Cade—is he a good kid?"

"Yes, surprisingly. Smart, too. And…he loves Jasmine. I'm not all excited about them getting married so young but they're determined." She gave him a pointed look. "You might want to keep that in mind when you tell Jasmine you have grand plans to invite her to check out Denver."

She started across the parking lot, her skirt swishing against her boots.

"When can we talk again?" Jonathan called. "When can I see my niece?"

She turned around, her hands on her hips and her

head tilted. "Come by the house tomorrow. We'll have lunch. Until then, stay away from her. Let me talk to her. She doesn't need to hear all of this from a complete stranger." She stood still, giving him another thorough glance. "I believe you know where I live."

Then she whirled with all the dignity of a queen and left him standing there. Jonathan hadn't even realized he'd been holding his breath until she was out of sight. He gulped in the cool night air, wondering what he would have done if she had refused to let him visit with Jasmine. And wondering why this particular woman made him bristle like a grizzly each time she looked at him.

Chapter Two

Arabella slammed the back door to the church kitchen, her mood shifting from confused to mad to sad. She shouldn't feel sorry for the man. It was ridiculous to hold her breath in awe against the person who'd spied on her, scared her silly and floored her with that bombshell of an introduction. But there was something about Jonathan Turner. Something that tore at her heart.

Maybe it was that haunted look of regret in his eyes or the way he'd put his hands in his pockets when he tried to explain things to her. Maybe he truly wanted to do right by Jasmine. And where was the harm in that?

He'd come here to find his niece. Now that she knew his real reason for being here, Arabella could let out her held breath. Only now she had a whole new set of worries.

One, Jasmine wasn't going anywhere with Jonathan Turner. Arabella was certain of that. Cade wouldn't allow it, either. He'd fight the good doctor on that one, same way he'd fought Arabella and his entire family on trying to stop them from marrying so young. Arabella had finally caved—her romantic heart overruling her pragmatic head. Jasmine and Cade were both adults now. They could live wherever they wanted and they could visit any city they wanted, including Denver.

And two, in spite of her sympathy for the loss of his brother and Jonathan's being alone in the world, Arabella didn't trust the man. She needed to learn more. Needed to see that he had Jasmine's best interest at heart. Arabella didn't cotton to shiftiness and lying, no, sir. The doctor had started off on a bad foot by not coming to her and explaining himself the minute he'd come into town.

And three, she didn't like the way he made her feel—kind of shaky and unsure, as if she'd stepped on a rock's edge and the foundation was about to give way underneath her feet. She was in shock, nothing more. Too much chaos would do that to a person, especially a person who thrived on order and routine. Her whole life had tilted over the past couple of months. For her kids' sake, she needed things to settle back down. This sudden development would not help, not at all.

First, her grandfather had gone and died on her just when she was beginning to truly understand him. Then seeing him on that strange video, demanding her cousins all come home and make nice by living in Clayton for a year so they could receive their proper inheritance. And now, a city slicker coming to town and announcing he was Jasmine's only living kin.

What else could happen?

Take a long breath, she told herself. *And say a long prayer.*

She entered the warm kitchen and went to work helping the bustling women finish getting the meal on the table. Staying busy was her way of blocking out all her problems. But when she carried out a big pan of baked chicken, Zach met her halfway and took it.

"Okay, so how'd that go?" he asked on a low whisper.

She shrugged, motioning for him to put the container on the table. "Fine...I guess. He seems sincere but I have to be sure. He wants to meet Jasmine. I told him to come by tomorrow."

"Want me there?"

She thought about that for a minute. "No. I think he can't be intimidated, even by you. And I get the impression he won't give up so easy."

"He has a right to know his niece, Arabella."

"Yeah, well, I have a right to protest that."

"Not a legal right," Zach reminded her. "But as a mother—a guardian of sorts—yes, you have certain rights. You've been taking care of Jasmine for a while now. Besides, from what I could find out, he's not married. Why would a bachelor want to deal with a niece?"

Arabella fussed with the silverware on the table. "I won't let him talk her into moving away."

"She's entitled to make up her own mind. She and Cade have been planning to move anyway. Or at least Cade's planning on going away to college."

"What if she does decide to go to Denver, though? What if she wants to leave for good?"

Zach patted her arm. "We'll deal with that if it happens. You've always said she was free to go if she wanted to. Don't go borrowing trouble."

Arabella wanted to tell her handsome cousin that trouble always had a way of finding her before she even thought of borrowing it. But a commotion near the entranceway to the fellowship hall caught her attention.

Zach started to speak again, but Jasmine pushed through the room and hurried toward them. "Arabella—"

Someone called from across the room. "Arabella?"

"Hold on a minute, Jasmine," Arabella said, turning. "Oh, great. It's Dorothy Henry. Probably wants me to serve on yet another committee." Dorothy ran the Lucky Lady Inn and kept her nose in everyone's business. She was always trying to fix Arabella up with eligible bachelors. "She's waving to me. I'd better go."

Zach shot her an amused look. "Better you than me."

Jasmine grabbed Arabella's arm, fear shadowing her blue eyes. "I need to tell you something."

Arabella's whole system hissed and buzzed. "What's wrong, honey?"

"That man is still here—the one we saw a while back. Remember he drove by our house and stopped at the corner? I just saw him outside again talking to some other people."

Arabella noticed the worry in the girl's blue eyes. *Had Jonathan already said something to Jasmine?* "Did you talk to him?"

"No, I came back into the kitchen before he saw me."

"It's okay. I've already spoken to him. I'll explain later. In private."

Jasmine didn't look so sure. "Maybe he left."

"I told him to leave, yes."

Dorothy shuffled in and headed toward Arabella, her cane hitting the linoleum, her patchwork purse swinging as she gave Arabella another frantic wave then called out, "We have a guest. And I especially wanted you to meet him."

Arabella waved back then turned to face Jasmine, hoping to distract her. "We'll talk later. Will you and Zach make sure we have enough coffee made? And we need ice for water and tea."

Zach pushed Jasmine toward the kitchen, then called over his shoulder to Arabella. "Go, go. We'll take care of the drinks. But remember, I've got your back."

"Good to know," Arabella replied as she looked back at him.

Then she turned around to find Jonathan Turner standing there with Dorothy.

"Found him in the parking lot," Dorothy said, smiling a bemused smile. "Told him to get on in here and have some dinner with us. And I especially wanted him to meet you since he went on and on about you and your bakery the other day." She glanced his way. "He loves your fresh-baked bread. Bought a loaf at the Cowboy Café."

Arabella's blood boiled over. He'd asked Dorothy Henry about her? Using her bread as a cover? "I just reckon he does love fresh bread."

Dorothy looked confused then leaned close. "He's a doctor from Denver. A single doctor."

Arabella swallowed back a retort and pasted a smile on her face. "The doctor and I have met, Miss Dorothy."

Dorothy put a hand to her faded yellow sweater. "Really now? Nobody told me that."

Dorothy had the idea that everything happening in Clayton had to come through her first. Weddings, funerals, births, breakups and especially new people in town.

Arabella glanced around. Thankfully, Jasmine had gone behind the swinging door to the kitchen. Zach motioned to that same door then went in, probably to keep Jasmine busy.

Jonathan looked as uncomfortable as Arabella felt. "We met briefly earlier out in the parking lot. We haven't had a chance to really get to know each other." Giving her an apologetic but challenging look, he reached out a hand. "Good to see you again, Mrs. Michaels."

Arabella took his hand, shaking it in spite of her better judgment. His grip was firm, his fingers lingering on hers while his eyes swept over her face. Did she see longing there in his misty eyes, a plea for forgiveness, maybe? Or was this just another one of his tricks?

The room turned from uncomfortable to a bit too warm.

"Call her Arabella," Dorothy suggested. "You two can't be that far apart in age."

"Arabella," Jonathan said. "I like that name."

"It means 'beautiful altar,'" Dorothy supplied with a beaming grin. "Or 'entreated,' depending on which name book you look at." She winked at Jonathan. "Of course, Arabella here's the one who'll have you begging. For more of that good bread!"

Dorothy cackled at her own joke while Jonathan looked like a trapped raccoon.

Arabella pulled her hand away. "It's almost time to eat. Help yourself, Dr. Turner." She turned to go back to her spot at the serving table.

"Excuse me." Arabella heard him, then noticed how he rushed past Dorothy, almost taking Dorothy's purse with him, to catch up. "I'm sorry. She insisted."

"I'm sure. Here to spy again? Pick everyone's brains for more information on my family?"

"No… I'm done with spying. But I would like to get to know my niece. And you."

Arabella turned on that note. "You should have tried that to begin with, by being honest. I don't trust sneaky people. And you'd better steer clear of Jasmine tonight. She's had a hard time of things, and I don't want to upset her. Not here, not now."

She glanced around and saw her cousins Marsha and Vincent across the way with Marsha's husband, Billy Dean Harris. Uncle Samuel's clan usually came to church when food was being offered, and they'd sure gossip about anything unusual. Especially if they found out Jasmine had an uncle from Denver.

"You can meet Jasmine tomorrow," she said, her tone firm.

He looked genuinely crushed. "I'd like to start

over, okay? Can we call a truce for now? I promise I won't approach Jasmine. I'll wait until you tell her."

"Since I don't have much of a choice, I guess I can agree to that. But…I'm watching you, you understand?"

"Got it. No more hiding in the bushes."

She looked him square in the eye. "Good, because next time I'll shoot first and ask questions later."

It didn't help that Pastor West held up his hand for quiet the second before she said that loud enough for several people standing by to hear.

And it sure didn't help that the good reverend chose that particular moment to ask, "Arabella, would you mind leading us in prayer?"

Jonathan found a seat across from Arabella, still smiling to himself at how she'd managed to go from threatening to shoot him to praying sweet words of praise and thanksgiving. He wasn't all that hungry, but the church ladies had ladled him a plate full of chicken and dumplings and fresh squash along with several other colorful vegetables, apparently grown in the community garden behind the church. They also piled on two big snickerdoodle cookies. He couldn't say no, not with Arabella Michaels giving him a daring look each time he thought about bolting for the door. He was afraid she'd either shoot him or pray for him. Or maybe do both.

To ease his discomfort, he pulled a worn picture out of his pocket, one finger touching the grinning face of the little girl. The picture was old. According to the lawyer who'd told him about her, Jasmine would be at least eighteen by now. All this time and he'd never even known she existed.

She was his only family now. They were both alone. Well, Jasmine seemed to have a solid church family. But he was all alone. He had a thing about family.

He'd always wanted a real one.

He wanted to let Jasmine know that he cared about her, even if his bitter older brother had stopped talking to Jonathan the day he'd left their sorry life behind. Jonathan wanted to offer her a chance to go back to Denver with him. Or at least come and visit him there. He could do that. He could give this girl the kind of life he'd never had.

He kept watching all the people laughing and talking around him as if they didn't have a care in the world. Arabella had introduced him to her cousin Brooke and a friend named Kylie, both nice women who'd offered him more food. Clayton had obviously hit on hard times, but no one in this room seemed to mind. Arabella told him they all pitched in to bring the food and that she supplied the bread and desserts for a lot of these meetings. Maybe there was something to being part of a church family.

But where was his niece?

"Want a piece of apple cake?"

He looked across the table at Arabella. She hadn't eaten much, either. "No, I'm good." He coughed. "I'm a little nervous. I can't get used to…being an uncle."

She leaned close. "I can't get used to you being *Jasmine's* uncle."

Seeing the tiny twinkle in her eyes, he relaxed. "I guess I could have knocked on your door and told you who I am."

"That's how most people announce themselves."

"What if she doesn't want anything to do with me?" he asked quietly.

Arabella scooted her chair around the end of the table so they wouldn't be overheard. "Are you kidding? That child is starving for love. I worry about her. She always sees the good in people."

"What if she can't see any good in me?"

Arabella leaned back and gave him a squinting look. "I can't see much bad, unless you're still hiding things from me. You could be a thief on the run or a bank robber passing through."

"Your cousin had me checked out, remember?"

"Oh, yeah. He did, didn't he? But…that doesn't mean I'm completely sure of you."

He quirked a brow. "Are you always this distrustful?"

"Yes, pretty much. I have good reason not to trust people."

He was about to ask her why when an older woman came walking toward them with three cute little girls, all holding hands. The woman wore her hair in a silver bun, but the little girls had shimmering, light brown curls and big pretty brown eyes.

Arabella stood up. "Uh-oh. Must have been some trouble in the nursery. Why is it always my three?"

Jonathan looked at the adorable girls then back at Arabella. "Your daughters? Dorothy told me you had triplets."

He'd seen her around town with the girls already. She obviously loved her children. And who wouldn't fall for these three? They were dressed in matching blue dresses with puffy sleeves and embroidery across the bodice. Each girl had a different flowery design, which probably meant their mother had recognized their individuality and made sure they did, too.

"Yes, four years old and growing too fast." Arabella nodded, then headed toward her girls, her smile at a thousand-watt beam. "Hello. Did you have fun eating your dinner with your friends in the nursery?"

"Jessie was mean to me," one of the girls said, pointing an accusing finger at her sister.

Arabella turned to the cute culprit. "Jessie, were you ugly to Julie?"

Jessie produced a pout. "Julie wouldn't share her cookie."

"Oh, my goodness. Julie, you know to share with your sisters." Then she turned to Jessie. "But, Jessie, you each had your own cookie, so I don't think you needed any of your sister's."

"I shared, Mommy." The third of the bunch said, her puffy blue plaid dress swirling around her chubby little legs. "I was nice to Jessie. I gave her part of my cookie then Julie gave me some of hers."

"Thank you for that, Jamie. But I think your sisters need to kiss and make up and then give you a big hug since you shared your food to please both of them."

The older lady laughed. "I couldn't get them to do that. They wanted to talk to you about it."

"C'mon, now," Arabella said, urging the girls toward the table. "Mommy has to help clean up. And I can't do a good job if I think you girls are mad at each other."

"Who's that?" Jessie asked, pointing toward Jonathan.

Arabella sent him an appraising glance. "This is Dr. Turner. He's here to…visit."

"No doctors," Jamie said, shaking her head. Her

sisters shrank back against Arabella, holding each other despite the cookie situation.

Jonathan couldn't stop his smile. "I see you're all acquainted with doctors."

"They don't like shots," Arabella said, mouthing the words. "This is a nice doctor," she told Jamie. "He came from a big city."

"Where?" Jessie asked.

"Not too far from here," Jonathan answered, the girls captivating him with their charm.

Arabella pulled at Jessie and Julie. "Okay, say sorry so I can get you back to the nursery for story time."

Jonathan watched as the tiny doll-like girls stared each other down then grabbed on for a long group hug. After that, they were all giggles. Arabella guided them back to the nursery worker, kissing each of them before they once again held hands and walked down the hallway.

"They're beautiful."

Watching them out of sight, Arabella turned back to Jonathan. "Thanks. They have their moments." She started gathering plates. "I'll see you tomorrow for lunch."

He got up, accepting that he was being dismissed. Accepting, but regretting it. He wouldn't mind spending more time with her and those little girls. "I'll help clean up, too."

"You don't have to. We have a meeting after cleanup. It's boring unless you're on the committee."

"Oh, right. Dorothy informed me I wasn't allowed to stay for that."

"She's afraid somebody will have better ideas than her," Arabella said under her breath. Then she put a hand over her mouth. "I shouldn't have said that."

"It's okay," he replied. "I've been around her for a little while now and I do believe you're right."

Arabella gave him a slight smile. "People are watching us, you know. Dorothy will be puffed up with pride, thinking she's made a match."

"Oh, is that why she insisted I attend this dinner?"

"You mean you didn't figure that one out?"

"No, I didn't. But… I'm glad she did force me in here. The food was great and it was nice to get to know you a little better."

"We'll see how that goes," she said. Then she turned and strutted away.

Jonathan told himself he didn't care what Arabella Michaels or anyone else thought. He'd come here with a purpose. He wanted to get to know his niece. And he wouldn't let a pretty, voluptuous woman in a flowing skirt and cute cowboy boots stop him from doing that.

* * *

Back in his car, Jonathan pushed at the memories of his own lousy childhood. In no hurry to get back to the Lucky Lady Inn, he made his way across the town green onto Railroad Street. Glad the speed limit was slow here, he let the top down on the convertible and breathed in the crisp fall air.

Just outside of the main stretch of town he stopped at the driveway of the huge creamy-yellow Victorian house with the big, tree-shaded yard. This was where Arabella, her triplets and Jasmine lived. He'd seen them at the town green when he had come to town the first time and followed them to this house.

A set of matching bronze-encased porch lights sent out a welcoming glow on each side of the big double doors. Colorful yellow and burgundy mums and fat orange pumpkins decorated the long wraparound porch, and a matching set of fall wreaths gave a welcoming look to the entranceway. Nice, he thought as he zoomed on by. It was a little rundown but still like something out of a magazine spread.

He hated that Jasmine had been abandoned. But he thanked God that she'd found a safe place to stay. And he couldn't fault Arabella because it certainly looked as if she cared about Jasmine. He'd just have to prove that he cared about his niece, too.

Driving around the quaint mountain town, Jonathan compared it to Denver. This threadbare little town certainly was quiet and less crowded, but it reminded him of the place where he'd grown up, which was only about twenty miles up the road. He didn't like small towns. This one held a forlorn look, like a frayed set of yellowed lacy curtains. But it also exuded a sense of pride. Apparently, Clayton had seen better days, but it wasn't a ghost town yet.

He sure hoped Jasmine would consider coming to Denver. Maybe she'd like the big city.

Pulling into the less-than-stellar white clapboard boarding house with the faded green shamrock-shaped sign proclaiming it the Lucky Lady Inn, Jonathan wondered for the hundredth time if this had been the right thing to do.

He'd made a nurse mad after canceling their date to take a few days to come down here. He'd also made the chief of staff mad when he'd told the man he might need to take an extra week to work this out. How would Jasmine react? Would his niece want to get to know him, or would she scorn him the way her daddy had?

Legally he couldn't force her away from a place where she'd lived her whole life. He was a complete stranger to this girl. But he wanted to be family to her. Jonathan needed this connection, needed to know that somehow he could make up for his past.

He might have to do that right here in Clayton. At least he could visit her here if she refused to come to Denver to see him.

He'd thought about becoming a family man a few times, and too many times he'd stopped himself. Most of the women he knew either wanted more than he could give or didn't quite need enough. He always managed to drive them away, no matter their own agendas. He'd never found the right fit. But having a niece might bridge that gap and give him some experience in the commitment department.

He couldn't wait to meet Jasmine. She was his closest living relative, after all. He wouldn't let the girl think she'd been completely abandoned.

Not the way his brother and he had been abandoned.

The girl might not have a mother and father, and in spite of all the wedding talk she had an uncle who wanted to get to know her and give her a better life. Jonathan made a good living. He could help Jasmine receive a college education, offer her a safe place to live, take her out of this one-horse town and show her all the possibilities of living in the big city. First, he had to get to know her and her fiancé better. And to do that, he'd have to get past that perky brown-haired guardian who wore flowing skirts and apparently knew how to use a gun.

Chapter Three

"What did you say to that man, Arabella?" Jasmine asked the minute Arabella got back from dropping the girls off at preschool. "Cade and I didn't stay to eat last night but I saw that silver car when we left."

"I found out why he's here," Arabella replied to Jasmine's rapid-fire question.

Yep, she knew why Jonathan Turner was here. Just thinking about the man had kept her up most of the night. He contradicted everything she wanted to believe about him. He'd gone about things the wrong way, but after talking to him she could almost understand his hesitancy. The man was single and a surgeon. Arrogance personified. Only he didn't seem all that arrogant. He seemed lost and lonely.

"Who is he?" Jasmine munched on dry cereal, her eyes wide with worry.

Arabella stared at her own cold toast, wondering the same thing. "He's a doctor from Denver."

"Why is he here?"

"He was looking for a family member." Asking God to help her find the strength to tell Jasmine the truth, Arabella closed her eyes and rubbed her temple with two fingers. "And…he's found that person."

Early-morning sunshine glinted through the kitchen windows, making Arabella wish she could enjoy the pretty fall day. She had to tell Jasmine the whole story, but so far she hadn't found the courage. Grabbing her third cup of coffee, she took another sip.

Jasmine tapped her fingers on the counter. "You know something, don't you? You're not telling me everything."

Arabella had to admire Jasmine's shrewd no-nonsense detector. "There is more…. Go get dressed and we'll talk."

Jasmine frowned then headed upstairs, the slump of her slim shoulders breaking Arabella's heart.

An hour later, Arabella sat with Jasmine in the kitchen. The old house was quiet, its bones creaking and shifting with a familiar kind of sway that usually comforted Arabella. But today it only added pressure to the tight fist holding at her heart.

"Talk to me," Jasmine said, taking Arabella's

hand in hers. "Is that man here to stop my wedding? Is this something about my daddy?"

Arabella squeezed the girl's hand, unable to speak.

Jasmine pulled her hand away, the tiny solitaire Cade had given her when he'd proposed twinkling like a baby star on her finger. "I won't give up Cade. I don't care how many spies Charley Clayton hires. I don't care if my own daddy comes back and tries to stop me."

Arabella winced at that declaration. "That man—he's not a spy, Jasmine. He's…he's your uncle."

Arabella hadn't planned to blurt it out that way, but the girl was about to hyperventilate.

"What?" Jasmine held a hand to her chest, her eyebrows lifting, her mouth widening. "What are you talking about?"

"His name is Jonathan. Jonathan Turner. He's a doctor in Denver and he only recently found out about you."

Jasmine sank down in her seat. "You're kidding, right? My daddy has a brother?"

"Honey, I'm not teasing you. I wish I were. And…there's something else you need to know."

The girl shook her head. "I can't take anything else. I can't believe he's my uncle. So he's here to see me, right? That's why he was following us and hovering around?"

"Yes, but he didn't mean to scare us. He only wanted to make sure he'd found you."

"Now that he's found me, what does he want with me?"

Arabella had to make Jasmine understand, but how could she when she didn't even understand herself?

"Honey, he had some bad news."

"What kind of news?" Jasmine backed away as if she already knew what was coming. "What else?"

"Your daddy...he died about a month ago. In a car accident."

Jasmine didn't move. She sat staring at Arabella, her mouth parted, her eyes vivid and bright, a raging river of doubt and shock. Finally, her voice cracked. "My daddy's dead?"

"Yes. I'm so sorry." Arabella reached for Jasmine but the girl pushed her away. "I...I need to talk to Cade. I want Cade."

Then Jasmine rushed out of the kitchen and straight upstairs to her bedroom, slamming the door behind her.

Arabella tossed her cold coffee in the sink, then stood staring out at the fall leaves in the backyard. She didn't want the girls to pick up on her tension. They'd be in preschool for a few hours, but what about lunch? She'd invited Jonathan to come here to meet Jasmine.

Deciding she'd tell their teacher to take them over to the Mother's Day Out program a lot of the moms in Clayton depended on, Arabella breathed a little easier. That would get her through this awkward lunch at least. Then she'd get the girls and settle into some afternoon baking.

But everything would be different by then. Although she didn't relish this new development, she squared her shoulders and decided to get on with things. Some changes you just couldn't stop or fix—like death or divorce or feuding families. She'd tried to fix all of those things and failed miserably.

"I need You, Lord," she said on a whispered breath. "I don't know how to deal with this. I'm tough and You've seen that. I never knew my daddy and I watched my mother walk away. I watched my husband pack his bags. I stayed by my grandpa, watching him die when no one else would help. I've tried to raise my girls the right way. But this—this is throwing me for a loop, Lord. I need You to help me get through this." Jasmine had come to mean so much to Arabella. She'd already been bracing for Jasmine's wedding and now this. She'd miss the girl, whatever Jasmine decided.

But after trying with all her might to stop the wedding, Arabella had a change of heart. Maybe because life was so fragile and unsure or maybe because underneath all her bravado, she still believed in love. How would the formidable Grandpa George have handled this situation? He'd probably hire someone to run the doctor out of town. But George Clayton hadn't been all bad. She remembered how he'd come into the hospital room when the girls were born. He'd stared down at the three little pink bundles without a word. But a single tear had fallen down his rusty old cheek. Then he'd turned and walked out of the room.

That tear had told her more than any words ever could.

Grandpa George loved his great-granddaughters. And he loved Jasmine, too. He'd want Arabella to fight for her home and for her children, including Jasmine.

Why had God allowed them to love Jasmine, to make the girl one of their own, only to bring Jonathan Turner here with bad news? Would he entice Jasmine with his wealth and position? Or would he promise her the moon but then leave and forget her? Jasmine had suffered enough.

Arabella had suffered enough, too. Was she being selfish, wishing Dr. Turner had never found his niece? Like it or not, Jasmine had grown up and was to be married in December. Arabella would have to let her go, one way or another.

Arabella had a hard time letting go, though. Her own mother had left her here in Clayton when Arabella, a teenager at the time, had refused to move away. She'd stayed for love, or so she thought. She'd married too young, and before she knew it, her marriage had fizzled out like a dud stick of dynamite. People were always leaving her, and she was tired of it.

What next? she wondered.

Outside, the leaves fell from the trees with a gentle abandonment that seemed to Arabella like a release. She wished she could just drift away like that. But she had responsibilities. She had to face reality. She couldn't let her protective feelings put a wedge between Jasmine and her. There really wasn't anything she could do, except pray that Jasmine would be happy, no matter where she wound up.

Arabella spent the next hour making soup and baking rolls for lunch. Only she didn't have an appetite and she couldn't get Jasmine to come downstairs.

Cade called Arabella's cell. "What's wrong with Jasmine? She left me a message, and she was crying." His voice filled with concern. "Is this about the wedding? Did somebody say something to her? I called back but she wouldn't tell me anything over the phone."

"Are you coming over here?" Arabella asked, hoping the boy could comfort Jasmine but dreading all that she'd have to tell him. "We can talk then."

"I'm finishing up some things with Mr. Jameson at the Circle C. I'll be over there when I'm done."

"That's fine," Arabella told him. Cade had big plans to become a doctor, but right now he needed a steady income and the Circle C ranch needed workers. Thankfully, Cody paid him a fair wage for a good day's work. "Come on over when you're done. I'll be here through lunch, so Jasmine won't be alone. Just get here when you can and maybe you can talk to her. She won't talk to me right now."

She was glad she'd told the girls' preschool teacher to take them next door to Mother's Day Out. Normally, she only sent the girls over there when she had deliveries or other appointments.

Their teacher, Mrs. Black, had readily agreed. "They'll be just fine, Arabella. The girls love playing with the other kids who stay late. Don't worry. Enjoy your afternoon."

Arabella didn't see how that would be possible. This was one of those day where she wished she could just run away and start fresh. But she busied herself with cooking, something that always soothed her when she was worried about things.

Her cell rang, showing Brooke's number. "So… what's up with you and that handsome doctor?"

"He's new in town," Arabella told her cousin. "And…he's Jasmine's uncle. His name is Jonathan, and he told me her daddy died a short time ago."

"Oh, that's horrible. How's she doing?"

"Not so great. I just told her this morning. Jonathan's coming over for lunch so he can talk to her."

"Give Jasmine a hug for me," Brooke said. "Listen, I heard from Vivienne."

Arabella braced herself. Had her cousin decided against coming home for the requisite year? "What did she say?"

"She's visiting friends in Denver right now, but… she lost her job. She said since she's got nothing to go back to in New York, she'll be home soon. She's willing to try the year thing."

Arabella thought how hard her vivacious cousin had worked to become a successful chef in New York. Vivienne hadn't been thrilled at the stipulation of having to return to Clayton for a year to receive her inheritance. But now she'd need that money. "Viv is being brave about this. I hope she won't regret it."

"I told her I sure am glad I came home, in spite of everything."

"Me, too," Arabella replied. "Thanks for the update. Now we need to pray Zach hears from Lucas."

"I'm on it," Brooke said before hanging up.

Arabella went back to her cooking, her prayers scattered from her cousin Lucas missing somewhere in Florida to Vivienne at loose ends in Denver and everyone in between. Especially Jasmine…and her uncle.

* * *

Jonathan walked up onto the inviting porch of what everyone called Clayton House. The big old Victorian looked pretty from a distance, but up close he could see the signs of wear and tear. The yellow paint was chipped and peeling in places and some of the big white shutters drooped with a heavy-lidded sway. This painted lady had seen better days. The house had to be over a hundred or so years old, so Jonathan took it in with a forgiving eye.

Maybe Arabella Michaels would be the same. Pretty from afar but worn a bit when he got up close. He almost wished that were true. Except last night she'd looked pretty good for a woman who'd come to confront him. He didn't need the distraction of a pretty woman right now. He had to talk to Jasmine, tell her he wanted to give her a chance for a new life and then get back to his old life. If he kept taking time off from the hospital, he could be out on his own, searching for a new place to work.

The front door creaked open with a groaning cackle. "I thought we agreed you wouldn't hide in the bushes anymore."

Jonathan gave Arabella a twisted smile. "I'm not hiding in the bushes. I'm right here in plain sight."

"Then why didn't you knock on the door? You've been standing there for at least five minutes."

He took in her careless chignon and the soft green sweater she wore over old jeans. And she had on yet another pair of cowboy boots—these a rich, burnished brown that matched her upswept hair. Unlike the house, she did not look worn and frayed around the edges. She looked great. All natural and all attitude.

"I...uh...this is hard," he said, his tongue tripping over his teeth. "I brought Jasmine a few things." He shoved the gift bag and a small bouquet of flowers toward Arabella. "The flowers are for you. And... some stuffed animals for your girls."

Arabella took the flowers and looked down at the big floral bag then back up at him, surprise and sweetness in her eyes. "I see you've been to the Flowers and Fancy Finds gift shop."

"Dorothy recommended it. And asked me several pointed questions about why I wanted to buy frilly gifts."

"I'll reckon she did," Arabella said, standing back. "C'mon on in. I might as well let you know—I told Jasmine everything and now she's locked in her room. Cade's supposed to come over in a little while."

Jonathan's heart knocked against his chest. "I didn't want it to be this way."

"She's upset about her daddy. In spite of Aaron Turner's nasty ways, I guess the girl still loved him."

"He wasn't always bad," Jonathan said, following her into what looked like a parlor. He saw antique sideboards and cherrywood tables mixed with a modern brown leather couch and high-back chairs strewn with colorful pillows. In one corner, a massive wicker basket filled with children's books and toys seemed to fit right in. Family pictures lined the bookshelves. "Maybe if I talk to her…"

Arabella pointed to a floral chair by the fireplace. "Have a seat. I'll bring in coffee. I made vegetable soup and bread. And I have pie."

"But—"

She whirled to stare at him, the big bag clutched in one and the flowers in the other. "I'm going up to tell her you're here. Maybe she'll come down." Laying the bag on a side table, she said, "And if she doesn't, well, you and I still need to have a long talk. So make yourself comfortable. This might take a while."

Jonathan sat down, nonplussed by her bossy attitude. He was used to bossing people around, but it sure wasn't as much fun to have the tables turned. He decided this trip wasn't going to be as short and sweet as he'd imagined.

Things were getting more and more complicated by the minute. And from the frown on Arabella Michaels's heart-shaped face, he had a feeling this was just the beginning.

Arabella found a crystal vase for the flowers. The fall arrangement contained vines and briar roses mixed in with fat burgundy mums and variegated sunflowers in amber and orange. It wasn't very big and it wasn't formal, but the cluster of flowers made a statement.

Was the man sitting in her parlor trying to make a statement, too?

She fussed with the arrangement and then put it in the middle of the long oak dining table. Jonathan's act of kindness had touched her. But then she figured he was making nice before he met Jasmine and plied her with big-city dreams. And why would a busy single doctor want to deal with a teenager anyway?

Maybe because that teenager was his only family?

Arabella could certainly understand that concept.

She heard footsteps and saw Jasmine moving down the stairs, her eyes red-rimmed, her hair falling in gentle brown ribbons around her face. Before Arabella could say anything the girl marched across the entry hall and into the parlor, stopping inside the arched doorway.

Arabella hurried after her but stopped in the dining area behind Jasmine.

"So you're my uncle?" Jasmine said it in the form of an accusation, the words sharp like arrows, her voice hoarse and raspy but determined.

Jonathan stood up, his hands going into the pockets of his jeans. "Uh…yes. I'm Jonathan. I'm sorry we had to meet this way." His expression was filled with a cautious joy, but his eyes held a definite sorrow.

Jasmine didn't say anything for a split second.

Then she crossed her arms at her midsection and said, "And so, my daddy's dead?"

Jonathan shot Arabella a helpless look and then focused on Jasmine. "Yes, he is. I'm sure you knew he was an alcoholic—"

"Yeah, I did know that. How did he die?"

Another pleading look. "He left a bar late at night and...apparently lost control of his truck on a curve." He started to say more but held back. Finally, he said, "He died on impact."

Jasmine raised a hand to her mouth then put her head down. "He wasn't always so mean. He just couldn't beat the liquor."

"I know," Jonathan said, his eyes burning with what looked like unshed tears. "I understand and I'm so sorry. He wasn't always like that when we were growing up, either."

Jasmine's head came up. "What made him get that way?"

"It was probably the disease." Jonathan stepped closer. "He followed our father's example, I think maybe to have something in common with our old man. They used to drink together a lot once my brother got older."

Jasmine swiped at her eyes. "But you turned out different? How'd that happen?"

He shrugged, his shoulders slumping, the weight of this discussion seeming to wear him down. "I tried to just survive. I...was younger. Aaron took the brunt of things. He wanted to protect me. I only wish I could have protected him."

Jasmine whirled toward Arabella and rushed into her arms. Arabella grabbed hold and hugged Jasmine tight, warning Jonathan away when he moved toward the girl. "It's all right. We've been through a lot together and we'll figure this out. It's gonna be okay, I promise." She voiced that promise loud enough for the man standing there to hear it.

Jasmine sniffed and looked up at her. "I always thought he'd come back here one day. That he'd want to come back for me. Or maybe he'd show up at my wedding. Now I'll never see him again."

Arabella held her own tears inside. It wouldn't do for her to fall apart, too. She had to be strong to keep Jasmine intact. "Maybe he was trying to get back. We can't be sure. Maybe he went away to get better and…just didn't have the strength to make it home."

Jasmine turned then, her eyes scalding Jonathan. "Maybe if he'd had someone to help him—"

"I didn't know where he was," Jonathan said, but it sounded like a pitiful excuse and he seemed to realize that. He dropped his hands to his sides. "I wish things could have been better between us. I tried to stay in touch, but he never answered my calls or my letters. He resented me going away to college."

Jasmine lifted her head an inch, her chin jutting out. "He used to pick on me about that. Said college was a big waste of time and money. Said I didn't have enough sense for higher education. I'd do better to get a job right here in Clayton and learn my place in this world." She held herself, her arms tight against her stomach. "I guess he was right."

Arabella leveled her gaze on Jonathan. "He was wrong, Jasmine. You're a very bright girl. If you want to go to college, we can make that happen."

And she dared the good doctor to dispute that.

Then Arabella had a new thought. Denver had several very good colleges. Maybe the doctor *could* actually help make Jasmine's dreams come true. And maybe it was time Arabella stopped wallowing in her own woes and, instead of resenting Jonathan Turner, found a way to help make that happen.

Chapter Four

"I don't have to go to college right now. I *want* to marry Cade," Jasmine said. "He's smart and he's looking for scholarships and working on securing student loans. He's gonna be a doctor like you. How about that?" she inhaled a tiny breath. "After we're married, he'd going to get started in college and I'm going to work to help support us. That's our plan."

Arabella saw the stubborn look on Jasmine's face. She wouldn't abandon Cade. And she'd put his dreams ahead of hers. The girl had talked about working while Cade went to college and on to med school. But neither of them had decided whether they should stay here and commute to any of the nearby large colleges or if Cade would live on campus. Either way, it would be hard to start a marriage like that.

Jonathan relaxed a little, a tight smile playing on his lips. "I...can talk to him, answer any questions he might have." Then he took another step. "How about you though? Don't you want to continue your education after the wedding?"

Arabella wondered if he'd accepted that there would be a wedding or if he was just fishing.

Jasmine nodded, the motion barely there. "Yes, I'd like to go to college, too. I've already checked into taking some courses online. But I don't mind working while Cade gets his medical degree." She shrugged. "I like cooking and baking. And there's no shame in waiting tables until I decide what I want to do."

Her tone indicated she'd be the one doing the deciding. Arabella was used to this but had to smile at Jonathan's poleaxed look.

Arabella touched her on the arm. "Let's talk about all that over lunch," she said gently. "Cade called earlier. He should be here soon. But we can go ahead and eat since it's ready. Your favorite vegetable soup and fresh-baked wheat rolls. And I made pumpkin pie for dessert."

Jasmine wiped at her eyes again. "Cade's coming?"

"He said he'd be here after he did some chores for Cody."

Jasmine glanced over at Jonathan. "He has a good job on a big ranch just outside of town. I told you he's smart and he works hard, too."

Jonathan focused on Arabella then glanced back at Jasmine. "I'm looking forward to meeting him."

Arabella motioned for Jonathan. He couldn't stand there in the parlor all day. "C'mon. Soup's getting cold."

He stepped across the hallway and into the dining room. The wall between the kitchen and this room had long ago been opened to form one long room that included the kitchen, a small desk and sitting area and the dining area. Arabella found it a bit disconcerting, the way Jonathan seemed to fill the space and make it smaller.

It had been a long time since she'd had company for lunch. Adult male company, that is. Why hadn't she bothered to put on some lipstick and comb her upswept hair?

Jonathan shot a wary eye toward Jasmine then asked, "Where are the girls?"

"They attend preschool at the church three days a week," Arabella said as she poured tea and ladled soup. "I sent them over to Mother's Day Out for the afternoon. I let them stay there some afternoons when I need to leave them with someone I can trust."

Jonathan took the iced tea she handed him. "You seem to have such a strong sense of community around here."

"We do. This little town might have seen better days, but we tend to stick together through thick and thin."

His guilty look made her wish she hadn't said

that. Did he think she was making a point with him? His next words explained that.

"I…we…grew up in a small town like this. It's about twenty miles from here, closer to Denver."

He didn't mention exactly which town, however.

"We like it here," Jasmine said, her words quiet but firm.

Jonathan smiled at Jasmine. She was busy placing bright yellow linen napkins around the table. But Arabella didn't miss the shy look Jasmine shot toward Jonathan. The girl was getting used to the idea of having an uncle apparently.

"Let's eat," Arabella said. "We have a couple of hours before I pick up the girls."

And so they sat down, the three of them. A minute of awkward silence followed, the only sounds the ticking of the grandfather clock in the foyer and the usual whines and groans of the old house.

Then Jasmine reached out a hand to both of them. "I'll say grace."

Arabella took the girl's hand on one side and then, reluctantly, took Jonathan's hand on the other. And the reaction she'd been expecting, the dread she'd felt coming since he'd shown up, settled over her like a rock slide, swift and accurate. Only now, the dread was mixed with a bit of anticipation, too. She had to inhale a breath to get her bearings.

Because she was holding the hand of a man who'd come here to mess with her carefully controlled, deliberately scheduled life. And that made him far more dangerous than she'd ever dreamed.

Jonathan took the coffee Jasmine handed him. Her tentative smile brought him a small measure of comfort. Was she warming up to him?

Jasmine placed a chunky slice of pumpkin pie in front of him. "Do you want whipped cream on top?"

"No, no," Jonathan said, eyeing the pie. "This is plenty. I'm not used to eating like this."

Jasmine glanced over at Arabella. "We always have plenty to eat around here. Arabella is a caterer. She bakes all the bread for the Cowboy Café and makes wedding cakes, too. She can cook for a big group, but you have to book that ahead of time. I help her. She pays me to babysit and help with the baking."

Jonathan saw the pride in Jasmine's eyes. He wanted her to feel that same pride about him. "Sounds as if you two have a good thing going."

Jasmine bobbed her head. "We do. Arabella's been good to me. She's like…my mom."

Bragging and making another point.

He wished he could accuse Arabella of taking advantage of his niece, but that didn't seem to be the case. Arabella Michaels didn't act like the type to work anyone too hard. She had a gentleness about her that belied the steel underneath. But she was a good person. He could see that from this cozy, colorful home and her unconditional love for her family.

He and his brother had never known that kind of love. Not after their mother had died when they were still boys.

Arabella wasn't taking advantage of his niece. She'd given the girl a home and a job. That was different from working the girl too much. And it wasn't the same—not the way his father had tried to work his brother and him, all the while making them feel somehow responsible for their mother's death. He was thankful Jasmine had found a good place to live.

But he needed to lay his cards on the table regarding his niece. "Now that we've had a chance to get to know each other, Jasmine, I wanted to extend an invitation to you."

Arabella stood straight up across the breakfast bar, the daring look in her golden-brown eyes nailing Jonathan to his chair.

"What kind of invitation?" Jasmine looked from him to Arabella. "I'd like to hear that."

He cleared his throat. This was the moment he'd been waiting for, the reason he'd come here. "Now that I know about you and I've seen…your situation," he began, hoping to make sense, "I'd like you to think about the possibility of coming to Denver."

Jasmine looked confused. "You mean for a visit, right?"

"No, I mean for as long as you want."

The girl pushed at her long hair. "But…you understand I'm getting married in December?"

"December?" He never dreamed the wedding would be that soon. "Isn't that a bit rushed? You've only been out of high school for a little while, right?"

"I graduated last spring. Cade did, too. But we both have jobs—just until Cade can get everything lined up for college and med school. And Arabella has a room here on the back of the house that Cade and I can use until we decide. It was her grandpa's room for a while."

Arabella came around the counter and sat down. "I had to move my grandpa downstairs for a few months before he died. After he passed, I remodeled the room and turned it into an efficiency apartment, thinking I might rent it out. It has a bath and a small kitchen. I offered it to the kids rent-free until they get settled and decide about college."

"So they'd stay here?" This time, Jonathan's tone *was* accusatory, but he didn't care. Maybe he'd been wrong to assume Arabella didn't have an agenda. "You've thought of everything, haven't you?"

Arabella gave him another stubborn look. "When my grandpa got so sick, all I could think about was that he didn't want to go to a nursing home. So I brought in a contractor to do some quick remodeling. We opened up a big storage closet and made it into a bathroom for him." She shrugged. "After he died, I thought about bringing in some extra income since my child-support checks are few and far between. So don't go guessing that I'm trying to manipulate things for my own benefit."

"I never suggested—" he began.

"I actually think it might be a good idea for Jasmine and Cade to consider living in Denver. Several fine universities are there and they have talked about that possibility." She met his eyes. "Having you nearby would ease my mind, that's for sure."

Jasmine bobbed her head. "That's true. It would be even better to know somebody in Denver. Especially a doctor." She glanced at Arabella. "Cade's mom lives there, but they're not close. He won't even talk about asking her to help."

Jonathan saw the hope in Jasmine's eyes and the encouragement in Arabella's.

Maybe she wasn't manipulating anything after all. But it would be hard to let her number-one helper leave. "Sorry. It just seems so convenient—wanting Jasmine and Cade to stay here with you."

Jasmine dropped her fork, her gaze widening.

"It's a good plan—if we decide to do that. We'll have privacy here before we decide about school. And if Cade goes on to college, I'll have a place to stay if I need it and he can come home on weekends. You have a problem with that?"

Jonathan saw that he was caught between two forceful personalities. He knew when to back down. "No, but I still want you to consider coming to Denver." He sent out his own challenge. "You and Cade both. As Arabella said, we have several very good universities. And I have connections."

Arabella put her hands on her hips and gave Jonathan a challenging look. "If you're willing to help them."

Jonathan tried to hide his surprise, still not sure if she was being sincere or sarcastic. But before he could stop himself, he blurted out, "Seriously?"

"Seriously," Arabella said, her expression a tad too smug. "That is, provided you'll stick around here for a while longer and get to know Jasmine and Cade, spend some time with them, let them tell you *their* plans. Get my drift?"

He got it all right. This woman wouldn't let go without a fight. That, or she was trying to call his bluff about letting them come to Denver. Well, that situation would definitely change his single lifestyle. Obviously, Arabella had already thought about that.

But he wouldn't be bullied into any type of commitment. "I can't stay. I have responsibilities—"

She leaned down, her hand centered near his half-eaten piece of pie. "Right now you have a responsibility to your niece. You came here to find her. Well, now you have. You can't just swoop in and grab her up and cart her off to Denver without talking about this and thinking things through. That's asking a lot, from us and from yourself. We both need to see if you have sticking power."

"Yes, we do," Jasmine said, nodding her head. "But, thanks for the offer, Uncle Jonathan."

Jonathan knew when he was outnumbered. "I guess I could take a few more days—"

The doorbell rang, followed by Arabella's cell phone.

Jasmine rushed to the door. "Cade!" She fell into the young man's arms. "You won't believe this."

Jonathan studied the young man. Muscular with dark blond hair. A nice all-American look. The kid pulled Jasmine into a tight hug.

"Are you all right?" Cade asked, holding her while he looked across the hallway and into the dining room.

"Come in and I'll tell you all about it," Jasmine said.

Oh, great. Another strong ally in their corner. Jonathan stood to greet Cade, hoping to get a handle on the kid's nature.

But before he could extend his hand, Arabella grabbed him, her phone in her other hand. "I need you."

Shocked and wondering what she had planned for him now, he turned toward her. "Okay."

"No, I mean I need a doctor. Julie fell out on the playground at church and busted her forehead. They think she needs stitches. Will you come with me to check on her?"

"Of course."

He turned and gave Jasmine and Cade a shrug.

"Go," Jasmine said. "I need to explain things to Cade anyway."

Cade looked confused, gave Jonathan a scathing look and then asked, "What's that man doing here?"

Jonathan gave Jasmine a reassuring glance as Arabella frantically dragged him out the back door and motioned toward her minivan. "Get in."

"I'll drive," he offered, seeing her agitation. "I have my medical bag in my car."

"I can drive. I'm fine."

Jonathan took the keys out of her hand, noticing the slight tremor. "Let me help. I don't mind."

She looked less than pleased, but didn't argue.

After he grabbed his doctor's bag and they were in her vehicle and headed toward the church, she finally took a long breath. "Thank you."

"I won't let you down," Jonathan promised.

She briefly locked eyes with him, then turned to gaze out the window.

He knew this temporary truce was the best he could get for now, all things considered. At least it was something.

"No sign of trauma to her head. She's alert and focused—no signs of shock. She'll be fine, but she might need stitches."

Arabella glanced from Jonathan to the curly-haired little girl clinging to her. "How many? Will there be a scar?"

Jonathan wasn't used to distraught mothers. He was a surgeon, and he mostly worked on adults. Children weren't his specialty. "I can't say how many but if you don't get stitches, she might have a tiny scar right underneath her hairline. We should get her to the hospital just to be sure."

Arabella got up, her hand pressing a wet towel against the still-sobbing child's head. "That's thirty miles away. Can't you do it?"

"Uh…I could but—"

"Look, she's bleeding all over this towel and I've got two more to worry about. Jasmine's with Cade, explaining everything, and Mother's Day Out is closing for the day. You're a doctor and you're here. You'll do in a pinch, won't you?"

He heard the frantic worry in her voice—and the doubt and fear. But she was right. "Yes…and yes."

He could break the rules. He'd given the little girl a thorough exam, and although her cut was minor, to her mother this still seemed like an emergency. Besides, it wasn't as if he hadn't broken a few rules before. "I guess this is a pinch."

Jonathan turned to where Mrs. Black sat in the big, colorful nursery with Jessie and Jamie and another helper.

When he motioned, the tall blonde came toward him, her eyes on little Julie. "I'm so sorry, Arabella. I was cleaning up my classroom when the MDO worker came running over from the playground. She thought I could calm Julie down. Poor girl turned her head for one second and Julie fell off the climbing rope and hit her head against the wooden ladder next to it."

Arabella heaved a sigh then kissed Julie's damp head. "It happens. We can't always protect them." She shot Jonathan a long look. "No matter what age they are."

"I can stitch her up but first I have to make sure she's in a sterile setting," he told the distraught teacher. "I need a room with a table. And a blanket to swaddle her. Arabella, I'll need both you and Mrs. Black to help hold her down."

Holding Julie tight, Arabella stood up. "Let's do it, then."

"Go on," the teacher said, waving them toward the room next door. "Our lunch table gets sterilized every day before we leave. I'll grab a clean sheet and blanket." She turned to the other worker hovering nearby. "Stay with the girls, okay?"

The young woman nodded and immediately went over to where Jesse and Jamie sat playing inside a big plastic toy house.

"Thanks." Arabella held the towel to Julie's swollen forehead. Then she turned to Jonathan. "Let's go."

Jonathan could see the fear in her eyes. "You sure about this?"

"Yes. Are you?"

"As you said, I'm a doctor." He'd taken an oath, so why was he so afraid? He didn't want to abandon her with a hurt child. He didn't abandon people. He just pushed them away. He wasn't afraid to do his job. He was afraid of failing at that job. But stitches on a preschooler? He could do that procedure in his sleep. This time, however, things felt different, as if doing this would be a test. If it meant gaining Arabella's trust, he knew he'd have to pass with flying colors.

They hurried to the other room. Mrs. Black put a clean white sheet on the long wooden table. She held up a blanket. "Will this work?"

Jonathan nodded then took off his coat. He brought his bag over and found the necessary equipment. "I'll need some alcohol to clean and prepare the wound and I'll need to give her a shot first to numb the area."

Arabella closed her eyes and bobbed her head.

He touched a hand to her arm then nodded to Mrs. Black. "Please put the blanket on the table. Then we'll swaddle her."

Julie realized through her sobs that something was about to happen. She thrashed against Arabella and drew close in her mother's arms. "I want Jasmine."

"It's okay, honey. Dr. Turner is going to make it all better."

Arabella gritted her teeth and pried the child's grip away from her sweater while Mrs. Black helped to lay Julie on the blanket. Then Jonathan quickly grabbed one end and tugged it around Julie. Before she could move, he secured the other side of the blanket and pulled it underneath her kicking legs. Soon, out of breath and sweating, he had her swaddled like a baby.

"Okay, now hold her arms down," he instructed the two women, speaking over the girl's sobs.

Arabella's eyes went a misty golden-brown. He gave her a reassuring look then got out a syringe. "She's not gonna like this," he told Arabella.

She nodded, one single tear moving down her face. "Just get it over with, please."

Chapter Five

An hour later they were in the minivan and headed home, the girls secure in their car seats.

Arabella turned around for the hundredth time to check on Julie, her expression still a bit shell-shocked and worried. Jonathan had guided her through the horror of having to hold her child while he sewed up her cut.

"Just talk to her in a calm tone. If you stay calm, so will she."

Arabella had handled the crisis like a pro. "Mommy's right here, suga'. It's okay. Just a little scratch. Dr. Jonathan is fixing you up."

Julie had locked eyes with her mother and listened to her soothing, loving words while tears rolled down both their faces. Jonathan would never tell Arabella he'd been almost as shaken as mother and child. He'd never given stitches to a four-year-old before or under such circumstances.

After he'd finished, he'd patted Julie on the head.

"Julie, you are one of the best patients I've ever had." Then he'd smiled over at Arabella. "You did great, too."

She'd only nodded, unable to speak.

"Thank you," she said to Jonathan now as she pivoted back around in her seat, her own memories evident in her autumn eyes. "I'm so glad you were here."

"You can stop thanking me now," he said, his smile indulgent. "Three stitches. Not bad for a first fall."

He could tell Arabella was still frazzled. The memory of Julie calling out "Mommy!" over and over had shaken him, too. And made him realize just how tough being a parent could get.

He was a good doctor. He'd shown her that today. And he didn't understand why it was so important to him that she knew that. Was it maybe because he needed to have her acceptance and respect and his work was the best way to achieve that?

She glanced over at him now. "Have you done a lot of this type of thing—stitching up kids, I mean?"

"No. I'm a general surgeon but I mostly work on grown-ups. I don't have to swaddle them."

She gave him a crooked smile. "We really need a clinic here in Clayton, but that takes money and influence. We have to rely on the regional hospital and its attached clinic for most of our medical needs."

Jonathan watched the traffic then turned onto her street. "It's not easy, having to drive so far to get to a doctor. Hope your ambulance service is good."

"Could be better," she said, turning once again to soothe Julie. The little girl hiccuped a lingering sob, her innocent eyes capturing Jonathan's in a tear-stained gaze through the rearview mirror.

Julie lifted a chubby finger toward him. "Who that, Mommy?"

Arabella smiled then stretched across the bucket seat and sent her daughter an air-kiss. "This is Dr. Turner, baby. He fixed up your boo-boo, remember?"

Jamie looked at her sister and then her mother. "I don't want stitches, Mommy."

"Me, either," Jessie said, patting Julie on the arm. "Julie cried."

"Don't want doctor," Julie said, twisting away in spite of her seat belt. "Mommy, hold me?"

"Just one minute, precious," Arabella said. "We're home now."

Julie let out a wail. "Hold me now, Mommy. Hold now."

She wanted her mother.

What child didn't? Jonathan wondered as they turned into the driveway of Clayton House.

It hit him that he, Jasmine and Arabella all had that in common. They'd each been abandoned in one way or another. Maybe that was why Arabella was so distrustful.

A little small talk with good ol' Dorothy late last night had provided a fount of information regarding the exotic-looking brunette. The chatty innkeeper had let it slip about Arabella's mother leaving her when she was a teenager. Apparently, Arabella had stayed in Clayton and gotten married, but her husband had also left her.

"Arabella's had a hard time of things. Sorry ol' Harry Michaels took off shortly after her triplets were born. Three of the prettiest little girls you'll ever lay eyes on, too. Man couldn't handle responsibility. Or so some say." Dorothy's eyes filled with scorn. "But me, I think old man Clayton paid Harry to leave. That old geezer was miserly to a fault, but rumor has it he had money to burn. I think he didn't like his granddaughter's no-good husband so he gave Harry the old heave-ho with a nice fat check to back it up. Either way, Harry Michaels is a deadbeat if you ask me."

That rankled Jonathan. He certainly knew about irresponsible parents, didn't he? And gossip aside, even if that kernel of knowledge gave Arabella a sympathy vote, Jonathan wasn't ready to concede all to the woman. Until today. Seeing her love for her injured child had cut deeply into Jonathan's own abandonment issues.

"A fine, upstanding woman, that Arabella

Michaels," Dorothy prattled on. "Glad you got to meet her and…since you're single…"

Yes, he was very single, but Jonathan hadn't gone into detail about that with the older woman. He didn't want his personal life to be the subject of the next circle meeting or quilting bee. Besides, relationships didn't work very well with his busy, hectic schedule at the hospital. And he had a few bitter nurses dogging him to prove that point.

He was known around the hospital as the love-'em-and-leave-'em type—or as his last girlfriend had said, "Turncoat Turner." Couldn't make a commitment, only in it for the chase—apparently all the clichés applied to him.

Jonathan didn't mind keeping it that way. He didn't mind being single. Even though he'd often thought of having a family, he really didn't believe in marriage and family because he'd seen firsthand how that could turn out. Or maybe he was just a big coward. But if he brought a niece to live with him, would his feelings change?

Arabella had practically dropped the challenge in his lap, hadn't she? She wanted to see if he had staying power. Remembering her tiny daughter crying out for her mom and for Jasmine, he wished he had someone who loved him that much.

And at least now he could understand the closeness of this little family. No wonder Arabella didn't want Jasmine to leave. The girl probably helped fill her own loneliness.

He stopped the car and got out to help Arabella with Julie and the other girls. Just one day with this woman and her children and already he was in too deep.

This trip had turned into more than he'd ever bargained for. But then, trying to make amends always came with a high price, didn't it?

Arabella remembered holding her daughter down, closing her eyes to the wailing sobs, while Jonathan gave Julie those three stitches. They might have wrapped Julie in a swaddling blanket to keep her from flailing her arms but she'd still squirmed and cried out for Jasmine.

"I want Jassy. I want my Jassy."

The girls thought of Jasmine as a big sister. How would they react if Jasmine decided to move to Denver?

"Hold on, baby," Arabella said now, gritting her teeth to her daughter's tired sobs. Unfastening seat belts, she said, "It's almost over. We'll get everyone inside and find some dinner." Arabella closed her eyes, her prayers asking for comfort and courage, for both Julie and herself.

But then, two strong hands covered Arabella's, the warm touch bringing her eyes open in surprise.

Jonathan.

"Let me help."

Unable to speak, she nodded, afraid she'd burst into tears from the sheer relief of having an extra set of hands. Male hands, at that.

He gently lifted Julie out of the car, holding on so the child wouldn't squirm too much. "I've got you, pumpkin. I won't hurt you. You're home now."

Arabella was right there, soothing her fingers over Julie's perspiring forehead. "It's all right, honey. Mommy's here. I'm right here. Time for you to rest."

Julie's little face twisted in protest, but she did seem to calm down a bit. Arabella leaned close. "See, it's not so bad. We fixed your cut. You hit the corner of the ladder when you fell. It scratched your pretty face. But it's okay. Just a tiny scratch. Dr. Jonathan is right here, too. See."

Julie gulped a giant sob then lifted her big brown eyes toward Jonathan. He bent down, his voice low. "Hey, there, pretty girl. How you doing?"

Julie burst into tears again, but Jonathan held tight. He gave Arabella a sheepish grin, but he never let go of her child.

Arabella turned away to help Jessie and Jamie out of the car, but she had to blink back the tears forming in her eyes. Why was she being such a big baby about this anyway?

Because he's being kind to you, nothing more. You're tired and weary and a stranger is being kind. She needed to remember she'd asked Jonathan to stitch up her daughter. But he would have done that without her prodding. She felt that in her heart. Gratitude wasn't the only emotion coursing through her frazzled mind.

And that part bothered her a lot.

"You'll need to keep an eye on those stitches," Jonathan said as they herded the girls up to the porch. "And make sure you put that antibiotic ointment I gave you on the wound."

"I will."

Julie reached out her arms to Arabella. Jonathan let go of the little girl, his gaze hitting on Arabella's as she lifted Julie into a firm hug.

Kissing her daughter, she whispered, "All better now, baby." She touched her fingers to Julie's riotous brown curls and gently brushed her hair away.

Jonathan's expression filled with admiration and longing before his gaze held hers. Arabella realized with a deep pang of regret that he'd probably never had anyone to soothe his pains or his hurts. And he still didn't have anyone.

"Thanks again," Arabella said to Jonathan a little while later.

The girls were playing near the toy box in the parlor, little Julie sipping on some juice while she sat watching her sisters. Jasmine had come rushing when they'd arrived, then listened when Jonathan explained what had happened. Now she sat near the girls, her need to protect Julie obvious while they waited for Cade to bring back the pizza Arabella had ordered over the phone.

Arabella sat with Jonathan across from the girls. He'd offered to stay a few more minutes in case Julie became fretful.

"I didn't do anything much so please stop thanking me," Jonathan said. He looked down, then fidgeted with his cell phone, his fingers scrolling down the messages. "How do you do this all day, every day?"

"Take care of triplets? Work? Worry?" She wondered that herself sometimes. "I don't know. I have a schedule and it works. It's easier now that the girls are older. It was rough there for a while when they were newborns. I've always thrived on order and control, but having three new babies blew that right out of the water."

He leaned up in his chair then reached for his coffee. "So…you're divorced?"

She gave him an impish smile. "You know I am. I'm sure Dorothy told you that right off the bat."

"Okay, she did. But if you don't want to talk about it…"

"Nothing much to say. Harry Michaels was a charmer all the way through school. I was sure in love with him. So much so, that I refused to leave town with my mama. She got in a big fight with my grandpa, then took off when I was sixteen. I didn't want to leave Clayton, so I stayed.

She shrugged. "Harry and I got married about a year after I graduated. My grandpa made me wait until I was out of school." Shaking her head, she added, "Things were great for a while, but Harry's charm didn't go away with our marriage. He liked to flirt a lot. He wasn't very responsible, either." She gave him a wry smile. "Not the best foundation for a marriage." She sighed. "We lived in a sweet little cottage out near Silver Creek, but Harry's work ethic, or lack thereof, caused us to lose that house. Next thing I knew, I was pregnant with triplets and married to an unreliable husband."

She stopped, slapping a hand to her mouth. "That was a lot of information for 'nothing much to say.' I'm sorry."

He smiled, his eyes crinkling. "I don't mind. Is that when you moved in here?"

She held on to her own coffee cup, her memories as dark and rich as the coffee. And even more bitter. "Yes. After a few years of marriage, I didn't want to depend on my grandfather, but this house sat empty for a long time. Grandpa traveled a lot, so since he was away and I had to figure out a way to help my babies, Harry and I moved in here." She sighed. "The babies came and Harry seemed to stay out more and more. If it hadn't been for my church,

I don't know how I would have survived. Then one night, Harry came home and started packing a bag."

She didn't go into detail about what he said to her that night, and Jonathan didn't press her. "Grandpa also was home with us when the triplets were born, but he never once told me I had to leave. He didn't talk much. But we had this unspoken understanding that this would always be my home. Now, I'm not so sure about that."

"Why? Are you having problems? I can reimburse you for Jasmine's care—"

"Don't insult me like that," she said, getting up to take his empty cup to the kitchen.

He followed her. "I want to help, do my part."

She should have told him he was way too late, but at least the man was trying. She'd give him points for that.

"I'm okay, moneywise. It's just—this thing with my grandpa's will. Each of my five cousins—my deceased uncles' children—have to live here in Clayton for at least a year for any of us to get our inheritance. It's an all-or-nothing deal.

"So far, Brooke and Zach have come back to fulfill their time and, surprisingly, they've both decided to stay here. And my other cousins Vivienne and Mei have tentatively agreed to this crazy plan, too."

Jonathan looked confused. "You have a lot of cousins."

"Yep. Vivienne is a chef—or was—in New York.

She lost her job so now she's in Denver, but she'll be home before the holidays, I imagine. Mei is hesitant but she won't let us down." A shadow crossed her face. "But if Lucas doesn't come home by Christmas, I might have to turn this house over to Cade's granddaddy Samuel."

"You don't think you'd be forced to do that, do you?"

"That's what the will stipulates. We can't even find Lucas. He lived in Georgia, but last we heard, he'd gone down to Florida and we think he's in trouble. Zach is trying to track him down."

"Maybe he'll come home soon," Jonathan said, his tone hopeful. "And as far as this house, didn't you take care of your grandfather when he was so sick toward the end?"

"Yes, I did."

"Then I'd say you deserve this house."

"But it's not mine to have, technically. Zach assures me no one will put my girls and me out on the street. But not everybody's like Zach. My uncle Samuel is just looking for an excuse to take this house. He wants it for the real estate, not the memories."

"You think the other Claytons would sell the house?"

"I hate to call my own kin bad people, but, yes, they'd want the cash. They're really bitter about this will. They think they got cheated, and maybe they did." She shrugged. "My uncle Samuel is a shady character from everything I've heard and seen. And some of his offspring inherited that particular trait."

She glanced toward the parlor and lowered her voice. "Cade somehow managed to get past all that. He really is a good kid and he's really smart. I guess he got that from his mama's side of the family."

Jonathan came to stand across from her, the counter between them. "Surely they wouldn't harm a mother and her children."

"You don't know these people. I'm worried they'll try to do something to keep Jasmine from marrying Cade. He's a decent person, but his daddy is a real rounder. He's been married and divorced twice."

"Maybe Jasmine and Cade *would* be better off coming to Denver with me after all."

Arabella had suggested that very thing, at first hoping to trip him up. But all things considered, it wasn't such a bad idea. Jasmine and Cade had planned to go away to college anyway—sooner or later. They could finally get the college degrees they wanted in Denver. And they'd be away from the influence of Samuel and his brood.

"Believe it or not, I really do agree with you there," she said, letting out a sigh. "But try convincing those two. I fought this wedding at first but they're in love and all they want right now is to be together, here in Clayton for starters. How they think they can manage that and jobs and an education, too, is beyond me. But I've changed my tune. Better to agree than to have them elope."

He tapped a hand on the counter. "When I get back to Denver, I can start making arrangements for housing and set the groundwork for both their educations. Between the two of us, we might be able to convince them to move immediately after the wedding instead of waiting."

"We just might," she said, her gaze meeting his. "But I still haven't figured out why a single, successful doctor would want to take on such a task."

He shook his head. "Neither have I, Arabella. But I have to try and make amends to Jasmine. That's my main focus right now. And if that means bringing Cade into the mix, then that's what I'll have to do."

Arabella could believe that. But the way the man looked at *her* told her he might have more than one reason for staying here awhile longer.

Did he want to bring Arabella into the mix, too?

Chapter Six

"All's quiet at last."

Arabella sank down on her favorite old leather chair, where Grandpa George used to sit and read in the parlor, then smiled over at Jonathan. "You didn't have to stay so late."

He got up. "I'm sorry. You're exhausted and I've been hovering around all day—"

"No, I mean I didn't expect you to stay all day."

He shook his head while she put her hand over her eyes, hoping to hide her embarrassment.

"I think this has been one of the strangest days of my life," he said, his expression edged with fatigue and a bit of amusement.

Arabella actually felt sorry for the man. "I can understand why. You meet your long-lost niece for the first time, then you have to do emergency stitches on a wailing four-year-old and help me feed pizza to triplets, then you're so tired you practically fall asleep waiting for me to get through bedtime and get them all settled for the night."

He sat back down and grinned. "Yeah, something like that. But I don't mind any of it—and I did offer to help with bedtime. I'm beginning to think life around Clayton House is never boring."

"Never," she said, relaxing into the chair, her bones aching for relief. He *had* offered to help with the girls, which was touching and thoughtful but also confusing. She still didn't get his motives. So she went on talking. "And tomorrow gets even better. I have six loaves of bread to bake and a wedding dress to finish."

His eyes widened in surprise. "Jasmine's dress?"

"Yes. My friend Kylie and I are trying to stick to a budget so I offered to make it instead of buying a more expensive version."

"I'd be glad to buy her a dress—"

"You don't have to do that," Jasmine said from the hallway. She walked into the parlor, her smile glowing with pride as she whirled to show off the simple wedding dress Arabella had made. "This one is perfect."

It was perfect, Arabella thought, but not because she'd made it. Jasmine made a beautiful bride. The dress was full-skirted, a creamy brocade with a pretty portrait collar that was both demure and sophisticated. Jasmine had picked the pattern to match a designer dress she'd found online. Kylie offered to make it, but she had her hands full trying to launch a new business. Arabella had stepped in hoping to extend an olive branch in support of the wedding. They'd made it together, stitching and measuring and laughing. Now all that was left was the trim work and stitching up the hem a bit more.

Jonathan stood back up, the look of awe mixed with pride in his eyes endearing him to Arabella.

"You look beautiful," he said, walking over to take Jasmine's hand. He twirled her around. "You're going to be a lovely bride."

"You think so?" Jasmine asked, dipping her head in a shy smile.

"Of course." Jonathan looked over at Arabella. "You made this?"

She waved a hand in the air. "Women have been sewing since the dawn of time, Jonathan. It's no big deal."

"I think it is," he said, letting go of Jasmine's hand. "I hear things around the hospital, nurses and patients talking. I know how expensive weddings can be. And most women demand fancy things—things with big labels and big price tags."

"Well, we're fresh out of both of those around here," Arabella said, getting up to fluff the dress and fuss with the beaded trim work on the collar. "We make do with what we have. I found these pretty pearl beads on one of my grandmother's old dresses."

Jonathan's smile softened his features. "You do more than make do. You seem to make things work. Better than most."

"I guess we do," Arabella said, touched that he'd noticed. She turned to Jasmine. "I think I'll tweak that beadwork a bit more and finish up the hem, but other than that, I'd say the wedding dress is ready. And that white wool cape you found in the consignment store will keep you warm and toasty until you get inside the church."

"It's so pretty, Arabella," Jasmine said, reaching out to give her foster mom a quick hug. "Thanks so much for helping me with the dress."

"My pleasure, sweetheart," Arabella said. "Now go get out of it and put it back in that protective garment bag for now."

"All right." Jasmine whirled toward the stairs. "I'm going to bed. Gotta get up early tomorrow and go talk to Deanna about getting some hours at Hair Today."

Arabella filled Jonathan in. "The local beauty parlor needs a receptionist and shampoo girl."

Jonathan stared after Jasmine. "Her daddy would be so proud."

"Just so *you* are," Arabella retorted, refusing to think about Aaron Turner and how sad his death was. Or how having his brother around made *her* heart twitch and flutter. "She seems to be warming up to you, so don't let her down."

"Let her down?" He looked frustrated. "I didn't come here to let her down, Arabella. I came here to show her that she has someone who cares."

"And so far, you're doing great," she admitted, hoping to soothe his agitation. "Really."

His frown matched his sarcastic tone. "I'm glad you approve."

"Are you?" She had to ask just to stir the pot and see how he reacted. "Do you actually care about my approval?"

"I think I do," he replied, gathering up empty paper plates and cups and heading to the kitchen. "I mean, it's only—what—our first whole day together, but already I can see that meeting your approval is important around here."

She followed him into the kitchen, hoping to convince him that she wasn't trying to fight. "It's not really me you have to worry about. It's Jasmine. I don't want to see her get hurt again."

He whirled at the trash can, anger making his eyes go dark. "Or maybe you're trying to tell me *you* don't want to be hurt again. Maybe you're afraid that I'll whisk her away and you'll never see her again."

"Maybe that is what I'm thinking," she countered, coming to stand across from him. "She means a lot to me."

"I can see that. I'd like her to mean a lot to me,

and I sure want to mean something to Jasmine. I'd like her to turn to me when she needs anything."

"You're talking about anything that money can buy?"

"No, I mean anything—all the things I never had."

Arabella saw the sincerity in his eyes and regretted antagonizing him. "I'm sorry. It's been a long day and I'm bushed. I shouldn't take it out on you of all people."

He came close, his eyes gray with their own brand of fatigue. "No, you shouldn't, but then, I'm the only one standing here."

"Yeah, and usually I just talk to myself, then go into prayer mode with God."

He smiled at that. "I'd say we're even. I have disrupted your life. And…you've certainly put a kink in my plans."

"So you agree you can't force Jasmine on any decisions. Whatever she decides has to be between Cade and her, although I do think you could be a blessing to them."

"Yes, I can help both of them. She seems very adult and very capable of taking care of herself. But…I'm not trying to compete with you or anybody else. I just want to be a part of her life."

Had he seen Arabella as being in a competition with him? Maybe she had been. And maybe he'd win out with all his talk of medical school and swanky apartments. But she had to abide by what Jasmine wanted, Arabella reminded herself. "I can live with that. You *should* be a part of her life. So… you're sticking around for a while?"

He looked doubtful then resigned. "I'm willing to do my part."

"Then you might want to consider moving into the apartment we were telling you about."

His surprise turned into shock. "You mean, here in Clayton House?"

"It beats the Lucky Lady Inn, don't you think?"

"Yes, but…wouldn't that be awkward?"

Wishing she hadn't blurted out the invitation, she bluffed now. "Not any more awkward than this whole mess has been from the beginning. We'll make do, Jonathan. And besides, I could use the rent money I'm going to charge you."

He laughed at that. "Of course, but won't people talk?"

"People always talk. You'd be renting an apartment with its own entrance out onto the back porch. We have lots of chaperones in this house. A teenager and three preschoolers and people coming and going all day long."

His gaze slid over her face, his expression changing from concerned to something more intimate. "Would we need chaperones?"

That whispered suggestion caused Arabella to blush and wonder what had come over her, inviting a good-looking man to come on in for room and board. "I don't know what you mean."

He pushed a finger through the wisps of bangs over her forehead, the touch causing her to shiver and grow warm. "I think you do know what I mean, but...I promise to be a gentleman. So I can win your approval."

"That's a start," she said, pulling away to hide the blush coursing down her face. "I'll hold you to that and I'll be watching you, Dr. Turner. Remember that."

"How could I forget?" he said, turning to head for the front door. Then he swung around to stare at her. "Good night, Arabella. Sweet dreams."

"Same to you," she managed to squeak. "Bring your stuff over tomorrow and we'll get you settled in. And...I'll make sure everyone knows why you're here."

"Yes, might be a good idea to do that. I don't want to get shot."

She smiled at that. "Good night and...thanks again."

He left, closing the front door with a gentle creak.

And leaving her with a gentle tear in her hardened heart.

Arabella woke with a giggle—her girls had been having a tea party with a handsome doctor in her dreams. Julie had served Jonathan cookies while Jessie combed his thick, dark-blond hair and Jamie poured tea, her brown eyes twinkling. A dream was one thing, but reality hit when she heard knocking at the front door. Boy, Jonathan hadn't wasted any time, had he?

Rushing downstairs in her button-up robe, her hair falling down around her shoulders, she wiped at her sleep-filled eyes and tried to make out the shape through the leaded-glass doors. It didn't look like Jonathan standing there.

Arabella fluffed her hair then opened the door, her expectant look turning to a frown. "Mom?"

"Hello, darlin'!" Katrina Clayton Watson stormed through the doors, her gold bracelets jingling a warning, her high-heeled boots clicking with precision. Then she turned to stare at Arabella. "Well, shut the door. That early-morning air is cold."

Arabella couldn't speak. What was her mother doing here? She hadn't seen the woman in ten years and had rarely received so much as a postcard or an email in all that time. Katrina hadn't even come home for her own daddy's funeral or the reading of the will. But then, she hadn't been listed in the will, either. She *had* sent Arabella a brief email, hinting that she might come for a visit, but Arabella had dismissed it as an empty promise. So why was Katrina here now?

Kat, as she always liked to be called, pivoted, her tight jeans and fake-fur vest making her look as if she'd been on a really bad hunting trip—in Vegas. "Don't I get a hug at least?"

Arabella raised her arms, the heaviness of this particular mother-daughter hug choking her breath away. "Why are you here?" she finally asked, her throat tight.

Kat stared over at her, taking in the lack of make-up and the disheveled hair. "You look like you haven't slept for weeks."

"I haven't," Arabella retorted, thinking her mother always did answer a question with a put-down. "I have three little girls, in case you forgot." Three little girls her mother had never met.

"I'm well aware of my grandchildren," Kat replied, dropping what looked like an I'm-here-to-stay-awhile suitcase on the floor. "Do you have coffee?"

Arabella rolled her eyes. "I can make some. I was still asleep."

"Asleep. How can you be asleep? It's almost six in the morning. I thought you always got up early to bake your bread."

Wondering why she should bother to explain, Arabella headed into the kitchen and started a pot of what she hoped would be strong coffee. "We had a busy day yesterday. Julie fell off the play gym at church—"

"Why do you force religion down those kids' throats?"

"—and put a gash in her forehead. Had to have three stitches."

"I mean, I know, I know, you have this Jesus thing going on, but where's that ever got you, huh?"

Arabella measured the coffee and started the brew, then put down the coffee can and squared her shoulders before she turned to face her mother. "What are you doing here, Mom? I mean, really doing here?"

Kat slumped against the counter, her big embellished black purse clinking and clanging when she slung it over a chair. "My daddy died and I heard he left specific instructions for all that money he kept hidden from the world." She snorted. "Trying to bring his family back together. That's a good one. The man never knew the meaning of the word *family.*"

Arabella figured it all out while she found cups, cream and the artificial sweetener her mother used to like. "So, you're here to make sure you get your part, even though Grandpa George didn't mention you in the will? Is that it?"

Kat brushed a hand through her teased red curls, causing her hair to rustle and settle back like a pile of dry fall leaves. "Mercy, no. I got my part of the inheritance when I left this creepy old house ten years ago, sweetheart." She came around the counter and poured herself a cup of coffee. "No, honey, I'm here to make sure *you* get your fair share of what belongs to you since you can't see the forest for the trees when it comes to George

Clayton. You just stand back and let me take care of everything, okay?"

Flabbergasted, Arabella put down her empty cup. "What are you talking about? Grandpa gave you money when you left?"

Kat bobbed her head then took a sip of coffee. "Yes, he did. Blood money. Paid me off to keep quiet…and forced me to leave without you. But believe me, that money didn't bring me a lick of happiness."

Arabella wished she could go back to bed and start over. "But…why would he do that? I don't understand. What did he want you to keep quiet about?"

Kat held her coffee mug with both hands, but Arabella thought she saw a tremor moving through her mother's skinny body. "Your grandpa wasn't a choirboy, honey."

"I never thought he was."

"He had secrets. Both of my brothers died in that horrible car accident. Am I the only one who wonders about that?"

A bubble of chatter came from the baby monitor sitting on the counter. Arabella looked over at her mother, wondering what she was talking about. "Mom, I have to get the girls. We can talk about this later." She definitely wanted to hear more about this story and why her mother was back. She hurried toward the stairs then stopped. "How long are you staying anyway?"

Kat gave her a smug smile. "As long as it takes, sweetheart."

Arabella rushed up the stairs, wondering how long that would be and also wondering why her mother was really here. Was it for redemption? Or had her mother come home for revenge?

Chapter Seven

Jonathan stood at the check-in desk at the Lucky Lady Inn, thinking for the hundredth time he should get in the car and head back to Denver.

He'd tossed around and punched his pillow all night long, trying to decide if he was doing the right thing by staying in Clayton. Jasmine was a levelheaded, smart young lady but she was rushing headlong into an early marriage. That worried him, but he had no right to try and stop her. He could give her his phone number and address then leave and let her make the next move.

Or he could stay and get to know her better and become a part of her life, including attending her wedding in December. And, he could get to know Arabella Michaels better in the process.

Did he want that?

Apparently he did. He couldn't get the woman out of his mind. And he didn't understand why. She was so different from the bossy, demanding nurses, drug reps and fellow female doctors he'd dated. Oh, wait. She had the bossy part down pretty good, but she did it in such a cute, feminine way that he never once felt as if he'd been cut off at the knees. He actually enjoyed sparring with Arabella. He was about to take that next step by moving into her house—the step that would force them to be together a lot more. Not sure of the wisdom of doing that, he signed the hotel receipt and gathered his suitcase.

"So, you're leaving us?" Dorothy asked from her perch behind the old counter, her ever-present lacy handkerchief tucked in the starched collar at her neck. "I thought for sure you'd stay awhile." Then she leaned close, her bifocals making her eyes look twice as big. "Especially since a little bird told me you spent some time with Arabella yesterday."

Oh, great. The rumors were already running amok. What would Dorothy think when he told her he was renting a room in Arabella's house?

"Actually," he said, choosing his words carefully, "I'm not leaving Clayton yet. I'm related to Jasmine Turner. She's my niece. So I'm going to be visiting with her for a while longer."

Dorothy sat up so fast she almost toppled off her stool. "You don't say. Well, now, why didn't I pick up on this obvious connection?"

Jonathan wondered how the shrewd old busy-body had missed that fact, too, but he didn't press the issue. "I'm just glad I found Jasmine. She's a sweet young lady."

"Yep, she is." Dorothy looked like a smug lady-bug, her eyes big and her cheeks puffy. "And…so is Arabella."

Jonathan couldn't deny his interest in Arabella, but he didn't dare tell Dorothy about his feelings. He still had to figure that out for himself.

"I'm grateful to Mrs. Michaels, too. She's been a good mentor to Jasmine. As good as any mother."

The old woman surveyed him with a thorough squint. "So where you staying, then? Found an apartment to rent or something?"

"Something like that," he said, turning to leave. "Thanks for the hospitality, Miss Dorothy."

"Don't mention it," the innkeeper said, her tone hollow with disappointment. Obviously, she was wondering where he was headed.

And so was he.

He made it to his car then heard his name being called.

"Hey, Dr. Turner, got a minute?"

Turning, Jonathan saw Reverend West hustling toward him. The robust minister waved a hand then pulled off his sunglasses. "You're not leaving town, are you?"

Jonathan took a deep breath. "No. Just changing locations. I've decided to stay awhile."

"Oh, that's wonderful news," the minister replied.

He hitched his pants up over his girth. "Listen, could we get a cup of coffee at the café? I really need to talk to you."

Wondering if Reverend West was going to try to get him to come to church, Jonathan almost declined. But…he'd skipped breakfast and he needed a jolt of caffeine before he settled into his temporary lodgings at Arabella's house.

"Coffee sounds good," he said. "Let me just get this bag in the car. The café's on my way, so I'll drive over. Need a lift?"

"Go ahead," Reverend West said. "I've got my car. Let's meet in about five minutes."

"I'll be there," Jonathan said, noting that the preacher had indeed driven here, so whatever he wanted to discuss must be important.

Jonathan got in his car and turned around toward the Cowboy Café, thinking if he'd left his car here Dorothy would probably wonder why he hadn't left yet. The woman had enough to speculate about as it was. And Arabella's house was on the other side of the small town anyway.

He found a parking spot across from the café and went inside. The preacher was already in a booth near the door, waiting.

"Hi," Reverend West said when Jonathan sat down. "I ordered coffee. Want breakfast, on me?"

"Sure," Jonathan said through a grin. "What's this all about, Reverend?"

The preacher motioned to one of the waitresses to bring two breakfast specials. Then he leaned forward in his seat and focused on Jonathan. "I hear you had to stitch up one of the Michaels triplets yesterday."

"I did." Jonathan figured the good reverend might be afraid of a lawsuit. Maybe he just wanted to make sure Arabella didn't serve him with papers since the accident had happened on church property. "She's fine now. Just three stitches for a cut near her hairline. It was an accident on the playground."

"So I heard," Reverend West said, waving to several of the patrons.

Jonathan glanced around and saw Arabella's friend Kylie Jones working behind the counter. He remembered being introduced to her at church the other night. He waved to her when she glanced up, then looked back at the preacher. "Was that why you wanted to talk to me?"

"Not exactly." Reverend West paused while the waitress put down their plates of steaming eggs, biscuits and bacon then took a sip of his coffee. "Well, first off, we have a church member who's sick and has little to no insurance. She's actually my secretary but...we can't pay her much."

"Why are you telling me this?" Jonathan asked, his tone patient even if he wasn't.

"She works when she can, only lately she seems

to be slipping away." After stuffing a few hunks of fluffy scrambled eggs into his mouth, he sat back to stare at Jonathan. "Well, son, I was wondering if you could go by her house and check on her. Just as a courtesy and a precaution."

Jonathan couldn't turn down helping a sick patient. "Of course. What's her name?"

"Darlene Perry." Reverend West finished off his bacon then slathered his biscuit with butter and strawberry jam. "She has advanced systemic lupus—complicated by other health issues. She's all alone and she has a ten-year-old daughter, Mary. The church has been helping her—you know, bringing food and helping with the girl's homework. Stuff like that. She can drive herself around town some, but she needs a doctor who can come to her."

Jonathan chewed at his own flaky biscuit. "Seems this whole town needs better access to doctors and health care."

"Yep, that's a fact. I guess you won't be here much longer though, huh?"

Did he dare tell the minister that he'd decided to stay a couple of weeks? Why not? He liked to stay busy and it wouldn't hurt to help out with a little pro bono work while he was here.

"Reverend, can I tell you something in confidence?"

"Of course."

Jonathan looked around to make sure no one was

listening. "I'm here for a reason. Jasmine Turner is my niece. I only found out about her a short while ago. My brother, Aaron, was her father. He died in a car wreck and a lawyer tracked me down because I was his next of kin, except for Jasmine. I'll be here a few more weeks, at least."

"I see." Reverend West pushed away his plate then placed his hands against the table. "Wow. That's tough. I assume Jasmine knows all of this?"

"Yes, sir. We visited yesterday. I was at Arabella's house when the day care called and said Julie had taken a fall."

"Good thing, too," the minister said. "Everyone at Mother's Day Out bragged on you. We could use a good doctor around here." He smiled. "So…since you're staying for a while, would you mind getting to know a few of our shut-ins? They could use a little encouragement."

"I'm not so sure—"

The chimes on the door behind their booth jingled, announcing more customers. Jonathan looked up to see Jasmine and Arabella, both carrying white boxes of various shapes and sizes. They breezed right by him without seeing him. But he couldn't help but notice how tired Arabella looked.

The stress of his presence? he wondered.

Reverend West grinned. "Speaking of your niece—Arabella and Jasmine provide most of the homemade goodies for the Cowboy Café and

Arabella donates her baked goods on a regular basis to the church." He rubbed his hands together. "We picked a good time to have breakfast. Fresh-baked goods. I'll have to take a snack for later."

Jonathan now understood why the reverend was built like a linebacker. He turned to glance back at Arabella and Jasmine, glad to be able to watch them do their work. They deposited several loaves of fresh-baked bread and a box full of pastries, placing their packages on the counter so Kylie could transfer the baked goods back to the kitchen. Jasmine smiled and spoke to several people, careful to hold on to the clear bag of what looked like double-chocolate-chip cookies.

"Hello," Erin Fields, the outgoing redhead who owned the café, called out from her spot behind the ancient cash register. "Just in time, Arabella. The natives are restless." Her silver earrings jingled right along with the bells on the door. "Jasmine, come on back to the kitchen. I'll show you where to put the bread."

Arabella gave her friend a wan smile while Jasmine helped Kylie put away the bread. "We got here as fast as we could."

Erin laughed. "I think you're getting more and more famous around here."

Arabella shook her head. "The Cowboy Café is the only place in town to get a good meal for a rea-

sonable price. So don't go giving me all the credit.
I just supply desserts and bread."

Jonathan could have listened to the exchange all
day long, but the minister cleared his throat, his expression full of interest and tolerance. "Dr. Turner?
About checking on some of our citizens?"

Jonathan glanced back one more time at Arabella.
She was busy setting her baked goods out on the
counter, her expression intensified by her work. She
sure had a lot on her mind but she kept right on
going. Maybe it wouldn't hurt to donate his time
and help out. "Uh…"

Reverend West shot a look at Arabella then back
to Jonathan. "C'mon, now. It'll do you good to get
out into the community. It's good you came looking
for Jasmine, but you can get to know other people,
too."

The reverend gave a broad smile. "Clayton's not
a bad place to put up a shingle. You might decide
you like it here."

"I doubt that…even though I agree everyone
here has been welcoming," Jonathan replied, getting back to reality. "I grew up in a small town, but
I didn't have a happy childhood. I prefer the city."
Why did he just tell the preacher that?

"So maybe it wasn't the town but the circumstances," Reverend West said. "You could change
all of that, you know. Coming here just might be
the change you need to make."

Jonathan thought about Arabella and Jasmine and those adorable little dimpled girls with eyes so much like their mother's. "Yes, I guess that could happen." He shrugged. "I can't make any promises, but while I'm here I don't mind doing a little volunteer work, I guess."

The reverend grinned. "I can make some space available at the church. Set up a classroom where you can meet with people."

Jonathan was impressed with the preacher's proactive nature. "That would be great."

"Then you'll visit Darlene?"

"Yes, sir. I don't have a problem doing that."

"Wonderful." Reverend West gave him the address. "She'll appreciate this, son. And so do I. Thank you so much."

Jonathan thanked the minister for breakfast then started to leave, Darlene's address tucked away in his coat pocket. He should at least say hello to the woman who would soon be his landlord, so he pivoted toward Arabella.

Arabella turned and spotted him but even while she looked unsure and fatigued, she held her cool. "Hey, there, Mr. City Slicker." She glanced over his sports coat and jeans. "How are you?"

"Good." He lowered his voice. "I was on my way to your house. How's Julie?"

"Fine. She's proud of her stitches." Her expression deepened into a frown. "About you coming to the house—I need to warn you…"

But a loud voice interrupted her. "Arabella, my customers have been bellyaching 'cause we ran out of your banana nut muffins. Got any of those inside that box there? And some of that sourdough-and-oatmeal bread, I hope."

Arabella smiled then told Jonathan, "He's one of the two cooks who help Erin run the Cowboy Café. But his brother and he think they run things around here."

Jonathan grinned. "Too many chiefs in this town?"

"Too many cooks in this restaurant." She turned back to the kitchen. "Of course I brought muffins, Gerald. Jasmine's putting bread on the shelf right now. Don't I always bring you a fresh supply every Friday morning?"

"You do and that's a fact," Gerald said, his hands on the white apron covering his ample stomach. "Let me go get the checkbook. We gonna go broke buying all your yummy stuff."

She gave Jonathan an apologetic smile and whispered, "He's the nicer of the two." Then she retorted to the cook with a mock frown, "You know you make a good profit on my baked goods. I might have to raise my rates."

"Now don't go and do that," Gerald replied as he waddled away. "Can't make ends meet as it is. This town is just about dried up."

From somewhere in the back, another man shouted, "Hush up, Gerry. You wanna scare off the few customers we got this morning? You're supposed to promote business—not lament about not having any."

"I ain't listening to none of you, Jerome," Gerald hollered to the tall, skinny man. "Get back to frying eggs. We got people lined up at the counter out here."

"That's the other brother," Arabella said through a giggle. "He watches every dime around here."

Erin walked by. "Just ignore those two. For some strange reason, they seem to think they're the ones who have to worry about keeping this place afloat even though I hold the purse strings, such as they are."

"They're cute and they love you." Arabella let out a breath and faced Jonathan again. "We can talk back at the house. Something's come up and you need to know about it. Meet me there and I'll explain."

"All right." Jonathan nodded then left the restaurant, all kinds of scenarios playing in his head. Had Arabella changed her mind about letting him rent the apartment? Or had Jasmine decided she didn't want her uncle around after all?

He'd just promised Reverend West he'd stay and help out, but if Arabella and Jasmine had decided against that, Jonathan would have to break that promise.

Chapter Eight

She wondered how she was going to get through this day. After dropping Jasmine off at the Hair Today beauty parlor, Arabella sat in her van and stared at her house. She couldn't believe her mother had appeared out of nowhere and was now upstairs with the triplets, cooing sweet grandmotherly words while the girls "helped" her unpack.

That, and the fact that Jonathan Turner was due here any minute to move into the guest apartment, caused her to groan and rub her temples. A major headache was forming right between her eyes.

She'd already put fresh linens in the closet in the guest room before she and Jasmine had left with deliveries. Then she'd found a pretty pot of mums out on the back porch to set on the desk in the big room. The bathroom was spick-and-span. Nothing to do now but wait for Jonathan to show up.

And to try and explain to him that her mother

was now also in residence here. The more the merrier, she thought. They say a full house made a full heart.

But in this case, it just gave her heartburn.

Hurrying to check on the bread she'd made earlier while trying to get over the shock of her mother's arrival, she opened one of the two industrial-size ovens she'd had installed last year and sniffed the smell of yeast and flour. The rough dough had risen to twice its size in the warmth of the big enclosed oven. Time to turn up the temperature so the seven-grain bread could bake to a nice golden brown.

Baking had always brought her comfort. She'd started right after her mother had left, and her hobby had now turned into a full-time business. Something about kneading the dough and watching it rise made her think of Christ and how He was the bread of life. Bread was indeed a comfort food. Maybe that was why people kept buying what she produced. Good thing they did because her baking skills paid most of the bills around here.

Hearing footsteps, she listened as her mother guided the girls downstairs. Even though her mother only knew the girls through pictures, Kat had insisted she could stay with them while Arabella made her deliveries.

"Now, your mama says we've got work to do. She

needs us to help with the baking. Do you girls ever get to play in the kitchen?"

"Uh-huh. Yes. We wuv bakin'." They all three answered at once, their cute little voices lifting up in a jangle of responses.

Arabella could at least smile at that. How many times had she dreamed of having her mother home and with the girls? How many times had she cried herself to sleep, wishing she had a mother who cared enough to come and soothe her frazzled nerves and her hurts and wounds?

Pushing away those tumultuous thoughts, she put on her serene face and waited for the girls and her mother to round the corner. "What's all this chatter about?"

"We're your new baking team," Kat said, her green eyes bright. "What do you need me to do?"

"Nothing right now. I turned the oven up so this batch can cook. Deliveries for today are made, Jasmine's talking to Deanna Stutz about a possible part-time job and…I have a few minutes to take a breath."

And try to tell her mother all the complications regarding Jasmine and her uncle Jonathan. But then, did she really want to go into that with her over-the-top mother? Kat had given Jasmine a cool reception when Arabella had introduced them earlier. Her mother would put herself right in the middle of things and probably make this situation a lot worse.

Kat grinned down at Julie. "We've unpacked every piece of clothing I brought, but I'm not so sure I'll ever find any of it again. The girls like to put away clothing in the oddest places."

"We helped Granny," Jessie said, her plump finger in her mouth. She sashayed back and forth on her fur-lined booties. "I got a necklace."

Arabella looked at the heavy beads around Jessie's neck. Each of her girls had a bauble. Julie wore a bracelet and Jamie had on a long gold chain. "Mom, those are nice, but we have to consider each as a possible choking hazard."

"Oh, for goodness sake." Kat reached for Jessie's beads. "Mommy says no, honey."

Jessie backed away. "No, Granny gave these to me."

"Uh, why don't you just call me Kat, baby?" Kat said with a grimace. "Granny sounds so old."

"Granny, you're not old," Julie said through a giggle.

Arabella held out her hand. "Let Mommy check on your jewelry and then I'll give it right back."

"No, Granny said we could wear it," Jamie said, her voice shrill and verging on tantrum level. "I don't want you to check."

"*Kat* gave them to you, baby," Kat replied, smiling as she helped Arabella confiscate the prizes. "Let me see if I can find something Mama will approve of."

Over wails and protests, Arabella said, "Mom, they can't call you Kat. I'd like to teach them to show respect."

Her mother made a face. "Okay, how about Grandmother Kat?"

"That's a lot to say," Arabella replied, trying to smile in spite of the tension sucking the life out of her.

"What do you suggest, then?" Kat retorted, her own smile stiff and stretched. Ah, there was the look Arabella remembered so well.

To stop the girls from whining, Arabella clapped her hands. "What can we call Grandma Katrina?"

"Really, Kat is fine by me," Kat said, this time with more force.

"Kitty Kat?" Julie asked with a grin. "I like Kitty Kat."

"Kitty Kat?" Katrina laughed out loud. "I like that."

"Kitty Kat, Kitty Kat," the girls said, singing the words through giggles, their despair from losing their new baubles now defused.

"I guess it'll work," Arabella said, shaking her head.

Jamie stood staring up at her flamboyant grandmother, her eyes centered on the bright green top and tight black pants Kat was wearing. "Pretty," she finally said, pointing to the gold necklace draped around Kat's neck. "I like that necklace, Kitty Kat."

"Pretty, yes," Arabella replied. "But you can't play with...uh, Kitty Kat's jewelry, okay?"

"Pretty? That's what you are," Kat said as she bent to grab the girls and draw them close. "Precious. So precious."

She stood, her eyes misty now, her hands touching on first one curly head and then another. "I've missed out on so much."

Surprised, Arabella blinked back her own tears. "Well, you're here now." She didn't push her mother to explain. Not in front of the girls.

"Yes, I am. So what's on the agenda? That bread smells like Heaven."

Arabella wished her mother truly understood Heaven and all it offered, but...she was afraid to break this fragile peace with any suggestions toward that end. Sharing her faith with Kat might prove to be as hard as making the girls understand this vibrant, gaudy woman was their grandmother.

She didn't have to worry about all that right now. The doorbell rang, its chime causing her heart to do its own answering echo. She'd hoped to prepare her mother for Jonathan's arrival. And do the same for him before he met Kat. Too late for that now. It was only nine o'clock, but this day seemed to be moving way too fast for her sanity.

"Who's that so early in the day?" Katrina asked, her head going up.

Arabella knew who was at her door. "It's my new

tenant. A doctor from Denver. He's renting out the downstairs apartment."

Kat stopped playing peekaboo with the girls and arched a shapely eyebrow. "What apartment? What tenant? Girl, what are you talking about?"

Arabella whirled as she headed to the door. "I'll explain later, Mom. Keep an eye on the girls for me. And…be polite, please."

"Aren't I always?"

Arabella didn't answer that question. Kat wasn't known for her impeccable manners. Arabella prayed that her outspoken mother would keep her mouth shut and allow Jonathan to get settled.

But how in the world was she going to explain this situation to Katrina?

"Hello," Jonathan said when Arabella opened the door. He had to admit that his stomach did a little dance at seeing her again so soon. She wore one of her usual long flowing skirts and a pretty frilly peach-colored blouse with a beige woven vest over it. Not surprising, she wore yet another pair of boots, these a rich baseball-glove tan. "Boy, something sure smells good."

"Bread," she said, waving him inside. "I have more orders to fill."

"So you sell to other places besides the Cowboy Café?"

"I sell and give it away wherever people like to

eat—church, other businesses around town, neighbors, you name it. I stay pretty busy."

Being a workaholic himself, he had to admire that. "Need any help?"

"Uh, no, thanks. I have more than enough help." She tugged at his coat sleeve, her eyes a rich goldbrown. Lowering her voice, she whispered, "What I wanted to tell you—my mother is here."

"Your mother?" That surprised him. "Does she live nearby?"

"No," she whispered, her eyes bright with worry. "I haven't seen her in ten years. She's here for an extended visit."

"Oh." Apparently there was still a lot he didn't know about this family. "I see."

Her eyebrows curved upward. "It's a long story and not a very pretty one."

Jonathan couldn't judge her. He had his own sordid family story, didn't he? "Okay. Just show me to my room and I'll be out of your hair."

"This way." They turned toward the back of the house.

And were stopped by a slender older woman with bright red shaggy hair and huge green eyes. "Aren't you going to introduce me to your guest, darling?"

Three little giggling, chattering girls rushed by and started pulling toys out onto the floor of the big parlor room. "Come play, Kitty Kat," Jamie said.

When she spotted Jonathan, she grinned. "Hey Dr. Jon-Thon."

Jonathan waved to the girls then glanced at the woman who stood sizing him up. "Hello."

Arabella shot Jonathan an apologetic look and said over the chatter, "Dr. Jonathan Turner, this is my mother—Katrina Clayton Watson."

"Nice to meet you," Jonathan said, maintaining a pleasant demeanor while he shook the woman's hand.

"Same here," Arabella's mother said. "Call me Kat—or Kitty Kat. The girls came up with that one. I was mighty surprised to hear my daughter is taking in a boarder. But now…I guess I can understand."

The look she gave Arabella spoke of a smugness and condescension that immediately made Jonathan wary.

That and the way Arabella's blush moved down her face in shades of pink and coral.

She was uncomfortable around her own mother.

And now she had him to deal with, too.

"Come on back and I'll show you where to put your stuff. I hope the apartment will be okay for you."

"I'm sure it'll be much better than the room I had at the Lucky Lady Inn."

"That place needs to be condemned, but Dorothy

won't hear of it," Arabella replied. "It's been in her family a long time."

"People seem to hold on to things around here."

They entered a room on the left side of the hallway. "Wow. This isn't half bad," he remarked.

The big room had a bay window looking out over the back garden. One side was a sitting area with a small, brown, aged-leather settee and matching high-back chair. A mahogany table sat between them. A big four-poster bed was centered on the other side of the room, and a dresser with lots of drawers and a small digital television sat nearby.

"The kitchen is behind these doors," she said, pulling back two folding doors to show an efficiency kitchen that contained a tiny stove and refrigerator and a few shelves on top. "And the bathroom is right through that door by the bed."

"It looks great. But I don't cook much."

"I'll feed you whenever you want." She gave the room a good once-over, her pretty blush belying her distant attitude. "This was a study and closet before we overhauled the whole thing. I hope you'll enjoy it. You're my first boarder."

Seeing the pride in her eyes, Jonathan lifted his overnight bag up onto the bed. "I'm honored."

"Well, make yourself at home then come on into the main kitchen. I have fresh coffee brewing."

"What a day," he said, smiling to ease the tension and to keep her talking. "I could use another cup of coffee. It's not even nine o'clock yet and already I feel like I've run a marathon."

"Yeah, what a day," Arabella replied. "I was just thinking that same thing earlier myself." Then she lifted her nose and let out a yelp. "Oh, no. I think my bread is burning!"

"Bread pudding? Seriously?"

Arabella nodded and continued scraping the charred black-brown crust off the ruined bread. She'd set the oven temperature too high, a sure sign that she was losing her grip. "I take this off and get down to the bread that's not ruined and salvage it. You ever had bread pudding?"

Jonathan twisted his expression into a questioning look. "I don't think I have. The only pudding I ever eat is that mushy stuff in the hospital cafeteria. And that's only when I'm desperate for some chocolate."

Arabella laughed in spite of the ruined bread. "So you like chocolate, huh?"

"One of my many weaknesses." He looked around then lowered his voice. "Uh…where did Kitty Kat get off to?"

Arabella rolled her eyes. "She said she wanted to go by Hair Today and get a pedicure. But I'm pretty sure she just wants to gossip with Deanna Stutz and the other women. So don't be surprised if she comes back with all the intimate details of your life."

"My life?" He grinned then started scraping the other loaf of bread, backing away as burned bits of crisp bread shot out into the air. "I don't have a life."

"Well, then they'll just make one up for you."

Watching as Arabella whirled to check the new batch of bread she'd managed to whip up, Jonathan once again admired the way she cruised through a crisis. She got frazzled but she held herself in check. Right now, the only sign that she'd had a busy morning was the bright spots of color dancing across her cheeks.

"Do you think people will talk about me, really? Just because I'm new in town and I happen to be Jasmine's uncle?"

"That and the fact that you're renting a room from me, yes. Too juicy to pass up."

He wondered what the good people of Clayton would think if they could read his mind right now. He sure wasn't thinking too much about his niece. His thoughts involved grabbing the breadmaker and dancing with her around the kitchen. The slow country song on the radio wasn't helping matters. Where were those little girls when you needed them for a distraction? Oh, right. They were settled down in the next room watching an educational video. Arabella had told him today was their day off from preschool.

"I don't want people to talk about you," he admitted. "I can handle it, though."

"Oh, so can I." She got out a big bowl. "People have talked about the Claytons all of my life. My granddaddy wasn't a kind man. After my grandmother died, he pretty much alienated everyone he knew, including his family." Glancing around, she shook her head. "I'm surprised he didn't put me out on the street."

He watched as she broke the bread into big chunks. "You seem to be holding your own. He probably admired your spunk."

She grinned. "Don't forget it."

He finished scraping then moved to help her, not really understanding why she seemed to be taking out her frustrations with each piece she threw into the bowl. "Do you make a decent living doing this?"

She didn't look up. "As you said, I'm holding my own. My ex does send checks but they come at random, so I can't depend on his timing. But I get by. And I love what I do."

She pushed at her hair with her arm. "But I have to be honest. I could use my part of the inheritance as a nest egg for the girls. Luckily, people are always hungry so my job is pretty steady. And now that Kylie is branching out into being a wedding planner, I think I'll have even more business. I have catered a meal here and there, with lots of help."

"Starting with Jasmine's wedding, right?"

"Unless we can find someone else more qualified but really cheap. So far, it's just a small tiered cake and appetizers at the reception."

"I can help with that. Just let me know—"

"I will, thanks."

He wondered if she *would* let him help, though. The woman's pride was as stiff and unyielding as the burned part of the bread she'd just scraped. "Why didn't you leave with your mom?"

"I told you, I was in love." She stopped with the bread then glanced over at him. "And…honestly, the woman drives me nuts. She's back for more than just visiting with her grandchildren. I think she's here to nose around about the will. She said my grandpa paid her off and told her to leave. I think she's back because she's out of money."

"You mean, she's interested in your share maybe?"

"Yes." She lowered her voice. "I wonder if my mother thinks she should get this house and my share of the inheritance."

"Good point. Does she know about the details of the will?"

"Yes. And I'm wondering how she knows. I called her when Grandpa died, but I didn't tell her about the will and she didn't come to the funeral or the reading. She emailed after he died and told me she might come to visit. That's the last I heard from her until this morning."

Jonathan finished breaking the bread into chunks and, because he wanted to make her smile, he asked, "Why are we doing this, by the way?"

She grinned over at him, catching him as he popped a big chunk of dark bread into his mouth then chased it with a swig of coffee. "I want the bread to sit a bit and get good and stale. Even though this is multigrain, it'll make a good bread pudding—lots of cinnamon and nutmeg."

"Stale? I thought stale bread wasn't good."

"It isn't, unless you're making bread pudding."

"And where did you learn how to make bread pudding?"

She finished the tearing and torturing of the bread. "My cousin Lucas sent me a recipe from New Orleans. I guess he went through there once on his way to Georgia. He raved about the stuff, so I tried the recipe and loved it. I've come up with my own variations, usually based on old or burned bread. Apparently, people down in the South eat it for dessert a lot, especially in New Orleans and along the gulf."

Loving the way she smiled when she talked about cooking, Jonathan kept her talking. "And what else goes in here to turn this stale bread into a wonderful dessert?"

"Eggs, milk, butter, sugar."

"Oh, all the bad stuff."

She looked up at him then. "Yes, all the bad stuff. Along with raisins and a few apples this time."

"I can't wait to be bad, then," he said, winking at her.

A blush spread over her entire face. "Look at the time. I've got to get lunch ready and then it's nap time. By the time I get all of that done, that second batch of bread should be ready to put in the oven."

"Want me to help with lunch?"

"No. I don't need you hovering around. Jasmine should be home soon anyway. You can have a nice talk with her."

She said it with a saucy grin, but he saw the underlying fear in her eyes. Did she feel the same way? Like riding the rapids and waiting for the big waterfall to take you downstream? Or was that just him?

"Meantime, you can just sit there and behave."

But he couldn't sit there. Soon, he was smearing peanut butter onto bread and opening applesauce containers while he made the girls peal with laughter at his exaggerated antics. Julie grabbed her cookie back and ran around the table, causing Arabella to frown.

"Okay. Enough clowning," Jonathan said. He pretended to steal their cookies and used his best Cookie Monster voice.

When he made a monkey face, Jamie followed suit then giggled. "Do that again, Dr. Jon-Thon." They all giggled and begged for more "fun with Doc Jon-Thon."

Finally, Arabella announced lunch was over. "Time for naps." She turned to him, her expression bordering on shy. "If you don't mind, I need you to watch the new batch of bread. It has to finish rising. Sometimes, it takes a while to settle them down for their naps, especially when someone gets them overly excited."

"Oh, you mean someone like me, for example?"

"Yes, you. So here's your punishment. She pointed to the stove. "If I'm not back in twenty minutes, turn the oven up to three-seventy-five and… please make sure it's set at that, not four-seventy-five like I did with the last batch. Okay?"

"Of course. If you trust me."

"I trust you. You don't want to see what will happen to me if we ruin another four loaves."

"Yes, ma'am." He nodded, deciding he'd have to be very careful not to burn the bread. Or upset the cook. "I'll keep watch until you get back."

After she'd corralled the girls up the stairs, Jonathan sat in the warm, sunny kitchen and listened to the quiet. He much preferred the chaos, he decided. It wasn't much different from an operating room. Only this room was filled with life and laughter and little-girl giggles, whereas he usually had to deal with life or death. His awareness of the contrast rushed toward him like a river, swift and enticing.

But he wasn't sure if he wanted to take the plunge just yet.

Chapter Nine

Jonathan was sitting in the kitchen reading a magazine when the front door opened and Katrina walked in with a proprietary swagger. "Hello, Dr. Turner. Still hanging out?"

"I'm in charge of the bread," he said, trying to be polite. For some reason this woman brought out the worst in him and made him want to protect Arabella. "She's getting the girls down for a nap."

"So she's got you slaving away in the kitchen already." Katrina put down her big purse then glanced around. "That child always did love to cook."

"Did she get that from you?" He lowered his head to hide a smile.

Kitty Kat missed the sarcasm completely. "Me? Ha! I burn water. Takeout is more my style. Or dining out—even better. Preferably with someone else picking up the tab."

Not knowing what to say, Jonathan got up to

check the bread. Then he glanced at the clock. "Time to turn the oven up and let it cook."

Katrina noticed the bowl full of crumbled bread. Giving it a cockeyed look, she waved her hand in the air. "Let me guess—bread pudding."

"Yes. Have you ever eaten any?"

"Once a few years back—I was in Texas at the time." She went all dreamy, her smile full of memories.

Jonathan allowed her a moment. "So you've never had any of Arabella's bread pudding, then?"

"Nope. She used to write me long letters, though, and in one of them she went on and on about this new recipe she had. New Orleans–style bread pudding. I never heard of such."

Jonathan didn't miss the sadness in her eyes. "She says it's really good."

"I bet it is. But I have to watch my figure."

He heard Arabella's boots hitting the stairs and breathed a sigh of relief. "I guess nap time went better than she'd hoped."

Katrina put down her water glass and stared at him. "How long have you known my daughter?"

"A few days."

"Really now? You sure seem mighty keen on doing for her, helping her out around here."

"Somebody needs to."

He was rewarded with a feminine scowl.

"You don't know the whole story about me, do you?"

"No, I don't," he said offhandedly. "And it's really none of my business."

"You are so right there."

Katrina turned and left the room without another word.

No, he didn't know the whole story but he sure had her number. And he wouldn't stand back and let her railroad Arabella. That much he did know. He'd only been around this place a short time, but everyone respected Arabella. He respected her, too. And he appreciated how she'd taken Jasmine in without question. So, yes, he'd stand in her corner any day. Especially if it meant going against this overbearing woman.

As seemed to be the case around here, when one door shut another one opened. Jasmine came through the front door and whirled into the kitchen just as Katrina exited onto the back porch.

"Uncle Jonathan! You're here."

Her youthful exuberance renewed his energy and erased any doubts he had about staying at Clayton House. "Yep. All unpacked and waiting on you."

"You been waiting long? I had a good talk with Deanna at the Hair Today salon. I think I'm gonna get the job as shampoo girl and all around gofer. And it's such fun to listen to all the chatter." She poured herself a large glass of orange juice and managed to take a breath. "You can learn a lot in a beauty parlor. Did you know Arabella's mom is in town? Does Arabella even know?"

Arabella came around the corner, holding a wicker laundry basket. "Yes, I know. She's staying here." She stared at Jasmine. "Did you get the job?"

Jasmine bobbed her head. "She's gonna call me later today, but I'm pretty sure—just have to get my schedule figured out."

"Good. I'm happy for you."

Jonathan gave Jasmine an encouraging smile, but Arabella searched the room. "Speaking of my mother, where is she?"

Jonathan tilted his head toward the back door. "She went out onto the porch."

Jasmine lowered her head to stare through the window. "That woman is kind of scary. She stayed on her cell phone the whole time Deanna was giving her a pedicure. And she was sure mad at somebody." She shrugged. "I don't think she likes me."

"My mother doesn't like anyone, honey. Probably on her phone now, complaining to somebody about something." Arabella opened the oven door to check on the bread. "A new boyfriend, I'm sure."

Jonathan took the laundry basket from her. "Where does this go?"

"I have to wash these clothes," she said, taking it

right back. "You already pay for room and board. You don't have to do chores, too."

Jasmine's gaze moved from her uncle to Arabella. "Let me take that."

"No. Jonathan has been waiting all morning to spend time with you. You two go—" She glanced at the back porch where her mother was pacing, smoking and talking on her phone. "Why don't you walk over to the park? When the girls get up, I'll meet y'all there. I could use some fresh air."

And apparently some quiet time alone, Jonathan decided. He looked at Jasmine. "Want to take a walk?"

"I guess so." She gave a shrug then grabbed a hunk of bread. "What's up with this?"

Jonathan grinned. "Bread pudding. I can tell you all about it."

"Oh, I know how to make it," Jasmine said. "It's really good. Arabella makes the best."

"So I hear."

He glanced back at Arabella, gave her a wink and then escorted his niece out the door.

Arabella went about her work, taking advantage of the hour or so the girls would nap to get some of her daily chores out of the way. She was in the laundry room sorting clothes when she heard her mother's raised voice out on the porch.

"I said I don't care about that. I need to know the

truth. I didn't come back here after all this time just to sit around and twiddle my thumbs."

What had Katrina gotten herself into now? Arabella wondered. Maybe she was looking for a job, too. Hoping her mother wasn't bringing trouble to her door, Arabella wondered if she'd have the gumption to kick her own mother out. She stopped, holding a pink T-shirt embellished with Dora the Explorer in her hands. Jessie's. Her little adventurer.

Arabella still had to pinch herself at times, the blessing of her children always front and center in her mind. She'd always wanted children, but having three at once had certainly proved to be challenging. But she wouldn't trade them for all the silver that might be left in the Lucky Lady Mine. Maybe she could use a bit more sleep most nights but she managed.

She'd manage now, she decided, even with her mother and a good-looking doctor in the house. Lifting up a prayer, she thought about how much Grandpa George had enjoyed seeing the girls every morning, even though he was too sick to do much more than lift a frail hand. He'd told her time and again, "You will always have a home here. Remember that."

Why had he said that when he knew his will would include stipulations? And what was her mother cooking up now?

She had a bad feeling that, whatever it was, it

had a lot to do with that infernal will. "Still causing trouble, Grandpa?" she whispered, her hands
clutching the little shirt.

The door around the corner from the laundry
room burst open and Katrina marched back inside,
the smell of smoke surrounding her. She looked up
at Arabella then wiped at her nose.

"Mom, is everything okay?"

"It will be, honey. It will be." Then Katrina
grabbed her purse off the kitchen counter. "I have
an errand to run. I'll be back soon."

Arabella didn't have a chance to ask her mother
where she was going. She wasn't sure she even
wanted to know. She started the laundry then went
back into the kitchen to take the bread out of the
oven and put away the chunks of broken bread.
She'd make the bread pudding to go with the pork
chops and steamed vegetables she'd planned for
dinner.

Through the baby monitor sitting on the counter
she heard little voices all talking at once. The girls
were up. Time to go to the park.

Jonathan heard them coming before he saw them.
He'd never stopped to listen to children talking and
giggling before, but now he found himself enjoying
the sounds. Arabella's daughters were beautiful—
just like she was—and they seemed to have their
own language, including hand signals and funny

facial expressions. He didn't know about their dad, but he'd never understand how a man could leave such a family. But then, he knew firsthand some men couldn't handle that kind of responsibility.

Maybe that was why he kept pushing aside his own dreams for a family. He was afraid he'd turn out like his old man. Look at what had happened with his brother.

But you don't drink.

No, he didn't drink. He would make sure he never did to protect any family he might have. Looking over at Jasmine now he made that vow again. His niece was warming up to him. They'd even had a long talk earlier about her upcoming wedding.

"Why do you want to get married so soon?"

"Because I love Cade and he loves me," she'd replied, gushing with pride.

"But…you're still young. You have all the time in the world."

"You never know about time, Uncle Jonathan," Jasmine murmured. "Nobody can promise that."

Who could argue with that kind of logic? "So how'd you and Cade meet?"

"At school. This bully was teasing me about… my dad and things. Cade stepped up and told him to get lost."

Who could argue with that, either? The kid had become a hero in Jasmine's eyes. Probably because no one had stood up for her before.

"Is Cade good to you?"

She bobbed her head then held out her hand to admire her engagement ring. "Yes, he is. He's not like his daddy. Charley is mean and lazy and barely has a job. Cade's the opposite." A faraway look filled her eyes. "He's sweet and caring. He wants to be a doctor so he can save people. He made up his mind to become one when his grandmother died. You haven't met his half brother Jack yet, have you?"

"No. I don't think I'll ever get around to meeting all of the Claytons."

"Jack McCord isn't a Clayton by blood. He and Cade have the same mama, though. Lorelei. She and Cade aren't very close. She lives in Denver with husband number three, by the way. Some say she married Charley for his name and money. Only he didn't have all that much money and, besides, he's not a very good father. Jack watches out for Cade, though."

"I'm still worried for both of you. It takes years to become a doctor. First, Cade will have to go to undergraduate school and then medical school if he passes the MCAT. Then he has to get through years of residency, usually with very little pay. Are you both prepared for that?"

She glanced over at Jonathan, the lift of her chin determined and sure. "You don't have to worry about us, you know. Cade took all the necessary courses in high school to prepare for college. And I did the same. We both planned to go to college even before we fell in love. So I really need you to help me convince Arabella that I'm gonna be okay." She exhaled a long-suffering sigh.

"She just wants the best for you."

"She thinks the same thing you do—we're too young, college is hard, working is hard. Cade and I are ready to create our own life, on our own terms. I figure life isn't so hard if you're the one making the decisions and being responsible." She shrugged. "I learned how to be responsible at a very early age."

Jonathan could certainly understand that concept. They had that in common. Most children of alcoholics had to learn that lesson, and a lot of them became overachievers for that very reason. "That's exactly what I did when I was your age. I left and never looked back. And it wasn't easy, but I did work my way through college and med school."

"See there. You're already an inspiration." Jasmine's smile was full of sweet contentment. But her smile faded on her next question. "Before you go back to Denver, would you go with me to my daddy's grave?"

"Of course." Ashamed he hadn't even been there himself, Jonathan couldn't refuse Jasmine. And he wouldn't leave her until they both understood that they were family now. "He'd moved back to where we grew up. It's not far from here. We'll ride over there one day soon."

"I'd like that."

So now here he sat remembering their earlier conversation while his niece whispered and cooed with her hero, Cade Clayton. Cade had called her a few minutes ago and she'd told him she was in the park with her new uncle.

"Do you mind, Uncle Jonathan?"

Why should he mind? He wasn't accustomed to being idle, but he had to admit this wasn't so bad after all. He could enjoy sitting here on a nice fall day watching young love take shape. In a little while he planned to drive the short distance to Darlene Perry's house and check on her.

But right now, he could think of little else than the simple pleasure of watching Arabella and her girls continuing up the street, hand in hand.

Arabella spotted him and waved. Then the girls saw him and were instantly at his side.

"Doc Jon-Thon, wanna swing me?" Jessie asked, always the first to get anywhere from what he'd seen.

Julie glared at her sister, her stitches covered with a protective piece of gauze. "No, he'll push me, right, Doc Jon-Thon?"

He got up, laughing at their mad dash to the swings.

Jamie, the quietest of the three, stood back with a pout. "What about me?"

"I think I can take a turn with each of you," Jonathan said, grinning as Arabella pulled up the rear.

She shook her head, her hands full of sweaters and juice pouches and a tote bag with teddy-bear designs on it. She sat her load down on the bench and met him at the swings. "I'll help."

"No wonder you're so slim and trim," he said, one hand on Jamie's swing and the other on Jessie's. "You have to keep up with these three all day long."

"I'm not in shape at all," she replied. "But I have a wardrobe that hides my flaws."

"I don't see any flaws."

She looked doubtful. "You know, you really need to stop trying to flatter me. I mean, you're renting a room in my house and you're helping me with the girls and you even offered to do laundry." Her voice softened. "Not to mention you're the first man who's ever helped me scrape burned bread. That's every woman's dream."

She stopped, her eyes widening as she realized what she'd said. "Not that I'm dreaming or anything. Just teasing you. Thanks for your help."

Jonathan hadn't gotten past the *flatter me* part. He'd like to kiss her and show her it was about more than flattering her.

Minutes later, acutely aware of her discomfort and embarrassment—and his own surprising feelings—he glanced at his watch. "Listen, I promised Reverend West I'd go and check on a church member. Darlene Perry? Do you know her?"

Real smooth, Doc Jon-Thon, he thought, but he did need to keep his promise to the minister. And now seemed like a good time to make a hasty exit.

Arabella looked even more confused and mortified. And a bit hurt. "Yes, everyone knows Darlene. I've taken her food several times. Her daughter, Macy, is a sweetheart. My cousins Brooke and Zach have gotten real close to her."

"Do you mind if I go and visit them, then? I called earlier and she said it would be okay to come by."

"I don't run your life." She kept her eyes on the three squealing girls. Then she finally looked at him. "It's nice of you to do that for Darlene. She doesn't talk about Macy's daddy much. In fact, Brooke has agreed to take in Macy if…after… Darlene dies."

He moved from pushing Julie on a swing to grabbing Jamie as she slid down the slide. Jamie laughed, then hugged his pant leg. "Swing me again." Jonathan helped her onto the swing by her sister. While Jamie swung and sang a cute little tune, he looked over at Arabella. "It's that bad?"

"Yes, that bad. The daddy's out of the picture." She glanced toward Cade and Jasmine. The couple was headed up the path to the swings. "Seems to be a pattern around here—dads who don't hang around."

Did she think he would be the same?

Jonathan wanted to tell her he wasn't that kind of man, but now wasn't the time. And maybe there would never be a good time. He wasn't going to stay around forever, so what did it matter?

But after he told everyone he'd see them later, Jonathan sat in his car and watched the scene in the town green. A pretty woman with silky brown hair and big golden eyes watched her three little curly-haired girls as they moved from the swings to the slides. A young couple strolled hand in hand and then joined the girls, chasing them and hiding between the rope swing and the climbing wall. The crisp fall air swirled and frolicked, the sun's rays trying to catch up. Somewhere in the distance he heard the crack of a ball against a bat and the cheers of some neighborhood kids.

A perfect fall day in a picturesque small-town park.

A very different scene from the many dark, miserable memories he'd tried to erase from his mind. His childhood, his town, his park had been nothing like this. He didn't even remember ever going to the park.

And yet he dreamed of having just such a family.

Then he started his car and took off down the street.

Chapter Ten

❧

"Okay, we want details."

Arabella glanced across the table at her cousin Brooke and their friend Kylie Jones. After Brooke's excited statement, they both sat staring at her as if they'd forgotten why they were here. They'd agreed to meet at the Cowboy Café to go over the details for Jasmine's wedding. It was a late Monday afternoon, a good time for all of them. The café was quiet right now so Erin had given Kylie a break from waiting tables and told her to take as long as she needed. Gabe Wesson, Brooke's new fiancé, was with his son A.J. Brooke took care of the little boy, but sometimes Gabe liked to spend some father-son time with the adorable toddler, even during a workday.

"You already have the wedding schedule. I think we've covered everything," Arabella said in answer to Brooke's question. "All children and significant others are accounted for. The bride and groom are together with my girls. What are you talking about?"

After discussing the plans and approving them, Jasmine and Cade had taken the girls for a walk so her wedding planners could get some things finished up. And Jonathan was on another visit with Darlene Perry.

"What kind of details?" she asked again, wondering if she'd missed something in her ever-changing schedule. She pointed to the to-do list open on the table. "Didn't I give both of you a copy of this?"

Kylie, now engaged to Arabella's cousin Zach, grinned and then poked Brooke, her green eyes flashing. "She's playing coy with us."

Arabella's gaze moved from Kylie's questioning expression to her cousin Brooke. "Do you know what she's talking about?"

Brooke tossed back her long blond hair, her one dimple deepening with her bemused smile. "It's all over town that the good-looking doctor from Denver is renting a room at your house. And the word is out about him being Jasmine's uncle. We saw him sitting with y'all in church yesterday, so we want details."

Arabella nodded, thinking she had no reason to hide anything. She just hadn't had a minute to tell her cousin and Kylie about the latest happenings at her house. But who was doing the talking? Probably her own mother.

Of course, sitting next to the man in church would only fuel the fire. Jasmine had invited him and then had conveniently left a place for Arabella to sit right next to Jonathan. No sense in trying to pretend he didn't exist.

"It's true. His name is Jonathan Turner, as you both know. I'm trying to keep things low-key for Jasmine's sake, but I should have known talk would get out after all the looks we got in church yesterday. I don't want Charley to make a big deal about it." Cade's grouchy father would try to make trouble, she just knew. "He's already hot under the collar about Cade marrying Jasmine."

"Why didn't you tell *us* the whole story at the meeting last week?" Brooke asked, her hand on her coffee cup. "And how long is he staying?"

"It just happened so fast. I first met him myself right before the dinner Wednesday night."

"Yes. He sat at your table," Brooke replied. "Gabe even commented on that. And Dorothy Henry went on and on about him. So that hunk is Jasmine's uncle?"

"You already have a hunk," Kylie reminded her with a gentle slap on her arm.

"I know that." Brooke had gone and gotten herself a good man, thankfully. Gabe Wesson was wonderful for Brooke, and Arabella was happy for her, especially since their cousin Vincent had put Brooke through the wringer when she'd first returned to Clayton. If Arabella didn't watch out, these two lovesick friends would play matchmaker to her, too.

Kylie tilted her head. "Zach was mum as usual about the details—comes with his job—but trust me, I noticed the newcomer, too. This sure explains why the new man in town kept glancing at you and Jasmine when you brought in your delivery Friday."

"He moved in the rental apartment that same day, right after you saw him in here," Arabella said. "I thought it would be good for him to be around Jasmine a lot." She clicked her pen shut. "I wanted to tell both of you more at church yesterday, but there was no time and…honestly, I'm still in shock. And the day I invited him to lunch to meet Jasmine, Julie fell at Mother's Day Out and had to have stitches. Dr. Turner stitched her up right there in the nursery."

She stared down at her notes, hoping she didn't sound too interested. "And so…Reverend West asked him to check on some of the shut-ins around here. He's visiting with Darlene Perry right now."

Brooke's head shot up. "I just talked to Darlene this morning. She never mentioned Jonathan Turner."

"He's only checking on her as a favor to Reverend West."

"That's so nice," Brooke replied. "Darlene needs all the help she can get these days. She keeps saying it won't be long now. She's worried about what will happen to Macy. But between all of us, I think that little girl will be okay. I intend to make sure of that."

Kylie's eyes widened. "That's for sure. But it's sad." Then she turned to Arabella. "Is Julie okay?"

"She's fine. Three stitches on her hairline. I'm sorry I didn't tell y'all any of this sooner. Between this wedding and finding out about Jonathan and everything else… I've been running in circles."

"You're forgiven," Kylie said. "And so is your stubborn cousin Zach. I tried to get him to tell me what was going on but he kept saying it was up to you to explain things."

"Which I have now." Had it only been a few days? Arabella wondered.

"Do they get along?" Brooke asked, her pumpkin muffin forgotten. "Jasmine and her new uncle?"

"So far." Arabella leaned forward. "But there's more. He came here because he'd recently found out that Aaron Turner was killed in a car wreck. Driving drunk. The lawyer told him about Jasmine. He didn't even know he had a niece."

Brooke gasped. "Oh, how awful for Jasmine. I'm so glad she has you and now an uncle, too." She tapped the table with her fingers. "And such an accomplished, nice-looking uncle from what I've heard and seen."

"Me, too," Kylie said. "He's been in here a couple of times. He's really a polite man. And he leaves big tips. He asked a lot of questions when he first came in, but I never connected on why. Amazing that he's Jasmine's uncle. Even more amazing that you managed to stay so calm about the whole thing."

"Let's get to the pressing question," Brooke said, eyeing Arabella. "Is he married?"

"No, he is not," Arabella said, bracing for what was sure to come next. "And, no, I'm not interested. Now can we get back to planning this wedding?"

Kylie pulled out her laptop. "Somebody's mighty testy today." She grinned at Arabella.

"Sorry. It's been a long few days and this week won't be much better." She didn't mean to sound defensive, but after that moment in the park the other afternoon, she couldn't pin any hopes on a romantic relationship with Dr. Turner. He was only here to get to know his niece. She wouldn't stand in his way on that. But she had been touched to see him sitting with Jasmine and Cade in church, considering he didn't seem all that faithful. Maybe she'd misjudged him on that.

Brooke gave Arabella a serious glance. "We're teasing you, but are you okay about all of this?"

"As okay as I'll ever be." Arabella took a sip of her hot tea. "It's been one surprise after another.

First, Jonathan Turner shows up, and then, bright and early Friday morning, my mother came knocking at my door."

"Oh, wow." Brooke gave Kylie a long glance, her eyes narrowing. "Tell her, Kylie. Tell her what you saw."

"I wasn't sure it was her because I haven't seen her in years, but you just confirmed it," Kylie said to Arabella. "I saw her Friday, talking to Pauley out in front of the town hall."

Arabella grimaced. Their uncle Pauley was the mayor of Clayton, but he hadn't done a whole lot to create growth or industry in the town. And he hadn't bothered with any goodwill toward her or her cousins since he'd heard about the will. In fact, he'd given Zach a lot of trouble now that Zach was the new deputy sheriff. "Why would my mother be talking to him? They always hated each other."

"Maybe he was welcoming her home officially," Kylie said, her tone dripping with sarcasm. "But I didn't see a Welcome Wagon basket in his hands."

"Or maybe he was letting her know he's not happy about the will," Arabella said, worry settling like river stones in her stomach. "I don't think she's too thrilled about it, either, but she won't talk to me." She didn't dare mention that her grandfather had paid his own daughter to leave town. She couldn't trust what Kat had told her as the truth.

Kylie made a hissing sound. "Speaking of—here comes Pauley and Charley now. And they look as thick as thieves."

Jonathan saw Jasmine, Cade and the girls strolling along the sidewalk near the town green. Delighted to see the girls looking cute in jeans and matching fur-lined boots, he pulled into a parking space and got out. "Hey, where are you headed?"

Jasmine waved, making sure the girls all stopped when she did. Over the shrill calls of "Dr. Jon-Thon," she said, "We've been taking a nature walk and now we're headed back to the Cowboy Café. Arabella's still there, working on plans for my wedding." She pointed to the excited girls. "We were supposed to go home for naps, but these three decided they really wanted some of Kylie's hot chocolate."

"Yes. Hot chocolate!" Jessie shouted.

He met them on the sidewalk. "Hey, girls." Then he shook Cade's hand. "How's it going?"

"Great. I'm on a lunch break." Cade still shied away from a real discussion, but at least the distrustful scowl was gone. Jonathan hoped to talk about the future with the kid if Cade would just relax and listen.

"What you doing, Dr. Jon-Thon?" Julie asked, her brown eyes glistening with gold flecks. She held up several leaves in various shapes and colors for his inspection. "Look what I found."

"I went to see a sick lady," he said, taking a maple leaf to admire it. "Remember I had to skip lunch with you and your sisters?"

As in, when he'd made a hasty exit this morning and had avoided the house because of his strong feelings for Arabella. Sitting near her in church yesterday had only reinforced those erratic feelings. Had he only known the woman a few days? Did matters of the heart really happen this fast? Maybe it had been the combination of her clean-smelling perfume mixed with Reverend West's message of being new again in Christ. Everything here seemed new and exciting lately.

"Did you give the lady stitches?" Jessie asked, one finger twirling a fat curl. "Did she cry?"

Jonathan wished it were that simple. "No, no stitches. She's sick on the inside. It's hard to fix."

"Maybe she needs a blankie and a hug," Jamie suggested, nodding.

Amazed that he was learning to translate four-year-old speak, he said, "I'm sure that would certainly help."

He couldn't say much more about Darlene Perry and her sweet daughter, Macy. But he did notice something interesting. All of Arabella's girls had the same one dimple, just like their mother.

And so did Macy Perry.

The little girl had blond hair and blue eyes and the one dimple like Brooke, Arabella's cousin. He hadn't noticed the resemblance when he'd visited Darlene and her daughter the first time, but it came to mind now. Macy had come home from school today as he was leaving, so he'd had an up-close look at her features.

Darlene had told him how, at her behest, Brooke and Zach both took Macy under their wing and helped her prepare for what was to come. Then the frail woman had confided what an incredible blessing it was to have Brooke and her fiancé agree to adopt Macy as their own when Darlene could no longer care for her daughter.

Jonathan couldn't help wondering if all of this was a mere coincidence. Or did Darlene handpick the Claytons as part of some grand plan?

"Let's go find your mother," he told the girls. As they strolled along, he put Macy out of his mind for now. He'd ask Arabella about his speculations later, though. "Why aren't you helping the ladies plan your wedding?" he asked Jasmine.

"I went over the details with them after I got off work from the beauty parlor," Jasmine said. "So they know what I want." Then she gave him a crooked smile. "Sometimes, my wedding makes me sad. I get overwhelmed and I have to just…step back and get away from all the planning. I wish my parents could be here."

Cade reached for her hand, concern in his eyes. "You have Zach and Arabella and…my family."

She smiled over at him. "I know. But…having your parents at your wedding is part of every girl's dream." Then she pushed a hand through her dark hair. "But…in spite of that, we are going to have a beautiful wedding."

Cade didn't look so sure. But he did look in love.

Her admission, spoken so softly, floored Jonathan. "I'm sorry, Jasmine…but I'm here. I'd never try to replace your dad, but I mean, if you want *me* at your wedding, I'll be there."

"That's good," she said, smiling. "Only, I already asked Zach to give me away. I didn't know about you when I asked."

Jonathan hadn't even thought about that. "It's okay. Just so I get to attend and see you in that pretty dress."

"Okay." She helped the girls toward the diner. "You can have the first dance with me, after Cade and I dance."

Jonathan looked toward Cade. The kid didn't talk a whole lot. "Good idea. That is, if it's okay with your groom."

Cade slanted his gaze toward Jonathan. "As long as I get the first dance. And as long as I get to go home with her."

"Then it's a deal." Jonathan smiled, relieved to pass that hurdle. He knew there would be many more.

"I guess that means you'll be coming back," Jasmine said. "I didn't think you would."

Jonathan realized he had to show this young woman he could keep his promises. He'd catch more flak about taking more time off from the chief, but no way was he going to miss Jasmine's wedding.

"Maybe if we pretend they're not there, they'll leave us alone," Kylie whispered to Brooke when Pauley and Charley paraded through the café doors.

Arabella took a deep breath. "I doubt they'll even notice *we're* here. They're both so full of hot air, they can't see anything else around them."

Erin tried to run interference by greeting the two men right away. "Hey, guys. What can I do for you?"

Pauley gave her a smug smile. "Two coffees and two slices of apple pie, sweetheart. Mighty quiet in here this afternoon."

"It's late," Erin replied. "The supper crowd will start rolling through in a few hours."

"Good, good. We need the traffic." Pauley flopped down on one of the old stools with all the grace of a leaping frog. "Me and my brother got some business to discuss." He whirled then stopped and poked Charley. "Look's like a whole pack of trouble over at that table."

Charley turned around and glared at the three

women. Arabella shot her cousin Brooke a warning look. "Let's finish up and get out of here."

Too late. Charley got up and came to stand over them. "What you three up to anyway?"

Arabella wasn't scared of the man, but she had childhood memories of his cruelty. "We're planning a wedding. A December wedding."

Charley turned red, the big vein in his neck throbbing purple. "You mean that farce of a wedding between my stupid son and that girl who's taking advantage of everybody in town?"

"No, she means the wedding between two people who love each other and want a good life together," Brooke shot back.

From his perch by the counter, Pauley hooted with laughter. "Them kids are too young to know how to make a life together. Pure foolishness." He sent Brooke a nasty look. "Just about as foolish as any man wanting to take up with you, Brookie."

Brooke shook her head. "You know, that kind of talk used to bother me, but Gabe loves me. And you'd better hope he doesn't walk through that door and hear you."

Charley bobbed his head, his thick neck bulging. "Ain't that the truth. We need that man's money in this town, even if his taste in women is questionable." Then he looked at Arabella. "And what's all this talk about Jasmine having an uncle come to visit? Did her no-good daddy send somebody to finally fetch her?"

Arabella felt Kylie's hand on her arm, but she didn't care. "You're behind on the news, Charley. Her daddy is dead. He died in a car wreck. Her uncle is her only living relative. He wants to be a part of her life. He'll be staying here in town awhile longer and he'll be at the wedding."

"Not if I can help it!" Charley said, his expression all puffed up and sure. "He'll figure out what everybody else around here knows. That girl is nothing but trouble. She came from nothing and she needs to go back where she came from instead of freeloading off everybody else. She just wants that Clayton title behind her name, is all."

"Now why would she go after the Clayton name when you all give it such bad publicity?" Arabella asked, her expression indicating Charley was first in line for that.

Charley shifted on his wide brogans, the sound of the bells on the doors causing him to lean down and get in Arabella's face. "You can say that again. Your grandpa did his own brother wrong, leaving everything to his grandchildren. My daddy should have inherited that fortune, including that old house you've set yourself up in, girly. Freeloaders, all of you. And Jasmine Turner is the first in line."

Arabella stood up, ready to tell Charley Clayton

exactly what she thought about real freeloaders, but a deep male voice stopped her.

"Why don't you step away from these ladies and let me worry about my niece?"

Arabella turned to see Jonathan standing there with her girls and Jasmine and Cade. Jasmine looked as if she wanted to cry while Cade stared at his father, shame and shock coloring his face. But it was the rage-filled look on the doctor's face that caught Arabella's full attention.

That cool, hard, smoky-eyed glare didn't bode well for the Clayton brothers.

Chapter Eleven

Pauley got up off his stool, his plate of pie in his hand. "You must be Jonathan Turner. Everybody in town is talking about the new doctor." Wiping pie on a napkin, he stepped toward Jonathan with an outstretched hand. "Nice to meet you."

Jonathan advanced into the diner then sent Jasmine a reassuring glance. He took Pauley's hand and briefly shook it. "It's good to be here with my niece." Then he locked his gaze onto Charley. "I'm thankful Arabella took Jasmine in and helped her out. Since my brother's death, I've been worried about Jasmine. But I know Arabella has her best interest at heart."

Charley grunted and went back to the counter. "You don't know much then, mister. But I reckon you've got more money than any of us, so you can at least take the girl off our hands."

Cade made a move toward his father. "You can

stop it right now. You know I don't like you talking bad about Jasmine."

Charley glared at Cade, his eyes bulging. "And you know you don't have any business marrying this girl. She's hooked up with the wrong side of the family."

Cade made another move, but Jonathan halted him with a hand on his arm. "Easy, Cade. Let it go." He pointed toward Jasmine and the girls. Cade glared at his father but backed down.

Arabella started gathering her things. "I need to take my girls home." She sent Jonathan a pleading look. "They don't need to be a part of this."

Julie, Jessie and Jamie looked startled. Each in turn rushed toward their mother, seeking protection from the tension in the air.

Kylie and Brooke got up, too. "I'm sorry," Kylie said to Arabella. "Maybe next time we should meet at your house."

"Good idea," Brooke said, her eyes on the two brothers. "I hope Zach doesn't hear about this."

The little girls looked from their mother to Jasmine. Jessie's big eyes moved over the two men at the counter. "Those men are scary, Mommy."

Pauley actually let out a hoot of laughter. "Nothing to be scared of here, little lady. I bet your mama didn't even tell you we're related."

Jessie stepped back toward Jonathan. Jonathan took the child into his arms then handed her to Jasmine. "Could you wait outside with the girls, please?"

Jasmine bobbed her head and gathered the protesting girls to get them out the door, promising them she'd make their hot chocolate when they got home. Cade shot one last look at his father then followed Jasmine, his face flushed and his head down.

Arabella glanced at Jonathan then hurried toward him. "Don't do this," she said, figuring he was about to have a showdown with her cousins. "They're not worth it."

Jonathan made sure Jasmine was out of earshot then glanced back at Arabella. "No, but she is."

He walked over to the two men. "Look, I don't know all the dynamics of your family dysfunctions but I can tell you this—my niece wants to marry Cade. I think they're way too young but because I just found out about Jasmine, I don't have any right to tell her what to do with her life. And Cade seems like a good person…in spite of everything." He exhaled sharply. "So I'm going to stay out of their wedding plans. I'd like to suggest you both do the same. Wouldn't you rather have them get married in a happy situation instead of having to elope?"

Pauley shrugged. "I don't really care one way or the other. They'll never make that marriage work."

Charley let out another grunt. "You're right about one thing, Dr. Turner. This ain't none of your business."

Then both brothers turned back to their pie, apparently dismissing Jonathan and the whole affair.

"Can we go home now?" Arabella asked, mortified that he'd been forced to get into her family troubles.

"I'm ready." He helped her with her papers, told Kylie and Brooke goodbye and then walked her out the door.

"Charming," he said, glancing back at her cousins. "I can see why you'd try to avoid family reunions."

"They're full of hogwash," she said, her voice strong in spite of her shaky pulse. "They always try to get a rise out of me and usually it works."

"Don't let them bother you. You've done a great job with Jasmine and your family, with no help from them it seems."

She let him take her tote bag while they walked to catch up with Jasmine and Cade. Arabella watched her girls up ahead. "I wouldn't want those two around my children. And wait till you meet *their* other offspring. Vincent and Marsha belong to Pauley. Vincent was engaged to Kylie but he was caught kissing another woman on their wedding day. Zach had come back to town and kind of ran into Kylie fleeing her own wedding. Even though Vincent tried to win her back and tried to mess with Zach, Zach and Kylie have been together for a few months now."

"Good for Kylie."

"Yes, but Vincent tried to make trouble for them. He thought he could bully Zach the way he did when we were growing up and he tired to get Zach in trouble. That's changed now. And Marsha is married to a man a lot like her father, lazy and without scruples. I try to avoid her because she brings out the worst in me."

"You don't have a bad side, do you?"

She grinned up at him. "You almost got to see it when you came in the café. Thanks for stepping up. I know Cade appreciated it. Poor kid. He only held back because it upsets Jasmine when he fights his own father on her behalf."

"You know, I still think they should come and live with me in Denver. It might help Cade to get closer to his mom, too. I'll get a bigger apartment or help them find one they can afford." He leaned closer, his eyes holding hers. "You did say you thought that was a good idea."

Arabella liked this man so she decided to be completely honest with him. "Yes, I'm beginning to think that truly might be the best thing for those two. Denver has everything they need to start their life together. And I meant what I said earlier about feeling better knowing you'd be there to help them."

He leaned close, his gaze holding hers. "But... you'd be all alone. Except for the girls, of course."

"I don't want to be selfish, so, yes, I'd be lonely

without Jasmine. She's a big help, no doubt about that. But I can find help. Lots of women around here need a job even if I can barely pay minimum wage. I'd just miss her because, well, I love her."

"She's easy to love."

The way he looked at Arabella made her wonder what Jonathan thought about *her*. Was *she* easy to love, or would he run the other way if he had a chance? And why on earth were her thoughts even going in that direction? The man didn't like the simple life, and he obviously didn't want a family of his own. Finding out he had a niece meant he had to come here and deal with things he didn't want to think about. He'd have to go back to Denver one day, with or without Jasmine and Cade.

They caught up with their little gang, giving Arabella a chance to clear her head.

While Jonathan took Julie's hand then somehow wound up holding hands with all the girls in a circle.

"Another long day," Arabella said to Jonathan, once he'd managed to free himself from the giggling trio. "Looks like my mother is home. She's up to no good…. I can just feel it. Kylie said she saw my mother talking to Pauley the other day. That can't be good."

"Well, they are related."

"But…they never got along and I'm sure they

haven't stayed in touch. Not that I know of, but nothing surprises me these days."

Jonathan gave her a doubtful look. "You need to make sure none of them takes advantage of your good graces."

"Thanks. I'm being careful."

She appreciated having someone on her side. She had Zach and Brooke and her other cousins Vivienne, Mei and hopefully Lucas, too. But it was getting mighty hard to maintain her cool with Samuel and his offspring trying to undermine everything she did. She wouldn't let them ruin Jasmine's wedding.

And she felt very strongly that Jonathan wouldn't let that happen, either.

"Mommy, can we please have our hot chocolate now?" Julie asked as she came running back to Arabella. "Jasmine said Miss Kylie couldn't make it cause she had to go back to work."

"That's true, honey. But I'll make it. We'll show Dr. Jonathan how good our hot chocolate is, okay?"

"'Kay." Julie smiled up at Jonathan. "You like hot chocolate?"

"Love it." He grinned at her then lifted her into his arms. "And I need a big mug full right this very minute. With a gazillion marshmallows on top." With that, he lifted Julie in the air as if she were an airplane, his mouth moving while he roared like a motor.

Arabella watched, laughing, as her two other girls rushed up to get in on the fun. Soon, they'd all been lifted in the air to be sailed around the front yard, their arms out like wings. Finally, Jonathan collapsed in a heap by the steps, his grin as big and wide as the golden-sweet sunshine to the west.

Cade and Jasmine, over the discomfort from their encounter in the café, dragged the giggling girls inside to start the promised marshmallows-and-chocolate party.

That left Arabella sitting on the steps, looking down at Jonathan. "You're just a big kid, aren't you?"

He stared up at her, his eyes crinkling, his smile intact. "I guess I am. I didn't realize that until I came here. I mean, it's been a long time since I acted like a kid."

"Stick around this house long enough and you'll be as silly as a stuffed monkey. We have fun day and night."

He gave her one more grin then his expression turned serious. "I'm beginning to see that. I'll miss those girls when I leave. And...I'll miss you, too. You have a real family, Arabella."

Arabella's heart turned to mush, reminding her of how her bread would go from flour and yeast and water to becoming soft and pliable in her hands. She was much the same when she was around Jonathan. That could be nice, if she didn't have a clear indication that he had a life to go back to in Denver.

But she couldn't help thinking the man could have a fairly decent life right here in Clayton, too. She almost said, "Don't go." But she didn't dare voice that request. It wasn't her place to tell the man what to do.

"I've got to get inside and start dinner," she said instead. "Even though hot chocolate before dinner will certainly ruin everyone's appetites. But since they've missed their naps, hopefully they'll go to bed early."

Jonathan jumped up to help her off the steps, his eyes meeting hers as he stood below her, holding her hand in his.

"I'm exhausted," he said, not making a move to get her inside. "I know you must be, too. Why don't we order pizza?"

"Pizza? We only have one place in town and it's local—not a chain. But it's pretty good. Same place we ordered pizza last week."

"I enjoyed that. So let me buy you dinner so you can rest and enjoy some time with the girls. Today was a whirlwind."

"Typical day for me." She pushed at her hair to hide the emotions erupting through her. "But you're right. We've had a lot of surprises today."

"So I'll help by providing dinner."

"You're my guest," she protested.

"I don't want to be treated like a guest."

"How do you want to be treated, then?"

He moved closer, so close she could see the reflection of the sunset in his eyes. "Well..."

The door burst open and Arabella turned to find Jessie standing there with her hand on her hip. "Mommy, are you coming? The milk is bub-bowling over and it's time to stir the chocolate in. Jasmine says you gonna have cold hot chocolate if you don't hurry."

"Yes, suga', I'm coming right now."

She let go of Jonathan's hand and rushed ahead of him into the house, the echo of her confused heartbeat trailing behind her.

"I think that doctor has his eye on you."

Arabella stared up at her mother then whispered, "Hush. He might hear you."

"He went to his apartment," Kat retorted, ice clinking in her glass as she gave Arabella a classic Kat eye roll. "So convenient, having him stay here. I think you and those girls wore the man slap out."

Arabella stifled a yawn then started putting away her sewing kit. She had Jasmine's dress on her lap, hand stitching the rest of the pearls onto the bodice. "He did have a long day. Reverend West asked him to go and visit Darlene Perry and today was his second visit. You remember her, don't you, Mama?"

Kat plopped down in the chair across from Arabella then looked out the window, her reply as soft and muted as the moonlit night. "Of course I remember Darlene. She's not much older than me."

"She has lupus," Arabella said, hoping to stir her mother away from the subject of Jonathan Turner. "She could live a few years or a few months."

Kat didn't seem to care. "So why involve Dr. Turner? I don't think he can do anything for her."

Shocked, Arabella closed up her sewing kit. "Mama, the woman is dying. I guess Reverend West wanted Jonathan to visit with her and try and make her feel more comfortable. She's broke, and her insurance has run out. It's the end of the line for her. She's already arranged for Brooke to be a mother to Macy when Darlene dies."

Now Kat looked shocked. She fidgeted on her seat and looked back out the window. "The little girl?"

"Yes." Why was her mother squirming like a rabbit? "You probably don't remember her."

"No, I don't think I do. Maybe that kid wasn't born until after I left." Kat got up. "I'm going to bed, honey. I suggest you do the same."

"What is it?" Arabella asked. "Did I say something to upset you?"

Kat shifted on her flower-encrusted mules. "I don't like that woman—Darlene. She tried to make trouble for our family long ago."

"Really? What did she do?"

"I don't want to talk about it. I'd rather talk about my adorable grandchildren and how that doctor would make a fine daddy for them."

Arabella got up, the bridal dress in her arms. "Honestly, where do you come up with this stuff?"

"I saw what I saw, watching you two out there on the porch earlier."

"You were spying on me?"

"I got eyes in my head, Arabella," her mother said, pointing to her temple with a long red fingernail. "I can sense these things. You'd better wise up and take advantage of what's right in front of you. Just think about it—you could move the whole brood to Denver and live the high life."

Arabella couldn't believe what she was hearing. "You want me to move to Denver with Dr. Turner?"

"It's not so far-fetched to imagine that."

"It is for me, Mama. I don't know the man well enough to even begin to imagine that." So far, she couldn't get past imagining what kissing him would be like.

"Well, get to know him. You need to leave this town, honey. It's depressing."

Arabella's shock merged with her own wayward thoughts regarding Jonathan. "He's a nice, attractive man, true. But I won't rush into something I might regret."

"You mean, the way you did the first time, with that sorry Harry Michaels?"

Why did her mother have a way of twisting every conversation back to Arabella's failures? "I didn't say that. If I hadn't married Harry, I wouldn't have my girls."

"Well, at least you got rid of him. That's a blessing."

Arabella thought about fighting fire with fire. She could remind her mother of how *she* got married young and sent her husband packing while Arabella was still in diapers. But that wouldn't matter to Katrina.

"I'm going to bed now," Arabella said, lifting the dress up so she could hang it on the hook out on the hall tree near the stairs. "Can you help me get this back into the garment bag?"

Kat held the dress while Arabella pulled the white plastic protective bag over it. "This is sure a pretty dress, honey. You did a good job on it. Want me to put it back in the closet?"

Arabella was so tired she couldn't think past getting upstairs and in the bed. "Put it in the hall closet for now. You might wake Jasmine if you take it into her room."

Kat did as Arabella said, then turned to face her. "Good night, sweetie. Think about what I said, okay?"

"Sure, Mama." Arabella planned to put her mother's wild suggestions right out of her head.

But once she was in bed and now wide-awake she

couldn't put Jonathan or the way he'd looked at her on the porch out of her mind. Her mother might be right about one thing.

Jonathan did seem attracted to Arabella.

And she certainly felt the pull of those gray-blue eyes.

But she wasn't ready to pack up and move to the city, and Jonathan had made it clear he liked living in Denver.

Impossible to dream about things that couldn't be.

And besides that, why would her mother push such an agenda?

Maybe because Katrina had her own agenda in mind?

Chapter Twelve

"Okay, I have a few errands to run this morning."

Arabella looked around her Wednesday-morning breakfast table. Kat sat helping Jessie with her toast and banana, while Julie and Jamie played with their oatmeal instead of eating it. Jasmine was reading a college course manual, her hand reaching out now and then for her apple strudel and coffee. Jonathan hadn't come in for breakfast yet. Maybe he was sleeping late or eating in his room. Staying in this house full of chaos could certainly make anyone tired. Especially one man in a house with six females.

"Is anybody listening to me?" she asked, wanting to get on with her day. She'd had another sleepless night.

"I heard you loud and clear," Kat said, making a face at the girls. "I can drop these little monkeys off at preschool for you."

"That would be great," Arabella said, not used to

having help other than Jasmine. Ashamed of herself for a jolt of doubt about trusting her mother to transport her children, she gave Kat a smile. "I'd appreciate it, Mama."

Kat reached her fingers across Jamie's purple sweater, tickling her. "Want Kitty Kat to take you to school?"

"Yes!" Jamie bobbed her head and her sisters were soon doing the same. "In your great big car."

"Then it's settled," Kat said. "I have some business to take care of myself. I can pick them up at noon when school's over."

Wondering exactly what kind of business her mother had, Arabella decided not to ask in front of the girls. The less she knew, the better regarding her mother's not-so-sparkling life. Besides, if she pushed Katrina for answers, her stubborn mother would clam up. That had always been the extent of their relationship. Arabella hated to shatter the gentle truce between them by asking pesky questions. But she should stay alert regarding her mother's comings and goings. This being a small town, she was bound to hear about Katrina's whereabouts.

"Thank you," she said to Kat. "I want to finish Jasmine's dress and let her try it on one more time. We'll make the final adjustments in December, but it'll be nice to have that project out of the way for now." She started clearing away the breakfast dishes. "Then I have to go to the general store for some supplies. I'm making a tiered cake for the Burfords' fiftieth anniversary."

Kat grunted. "The Burfords! Are they still alive? They were old when I was a teenager."

"Still alive and kicking," Arabella replied. "And still in love as hard as that is to imagine."

"Yep. Not like you and me, suga'. We tend to send men packing."

Arabella shot her mother a warning look. "Not in front of the…"

Kat clamped a hand over her mouth. "I have to remember little ears listen big."

"Little ears, little ears," Julie chanted, grinning at her sisters. "I have little ears, Kitty Kat."

"I can see your ears," Kat replied, quickly making a game out of finding all of the girls' ears.

Jasmine finished her strudel and absently kissed Arabella then turned to snuggle with each of the triplets. Giving Kat a wide berth, she called out, "Gotta go. My first full day at Hair Today." She turned back at the arched opening to the hallway. "Arabella, I'll be working from nine until three. That way I can still help you with packaging whatever you bake today. And I'll take Triplet Watch when I get home."

"Thanks, honey," Arabella said, laughing at Jasmine's name for babysitting duties. "I've got all the bread ready for the oven, and I'll get the pastries and pies done while the girls are at school. I just have to get a few ingredients this morning and run some other errands."

After Jasmine left, Kat helped Arabella get the girls into their jackets. "I'll be done in time to pick them up," Kat reminded her. "Take your time with your errands."

Arabella helped her mother get the girls in the backseat of her car, the three car seats sitting snugly together. She waved to them as Kat pulled out onto the street, her late-model Cadillac clanking and clunking. Her mother had always gone for showy and impressive rather than practical and passable.

Shaking her head at that, Arabella headed back inside, the early-morning chill reminding her that winter would be here soon. That meant more colds and other ailments, which meant doctor bills to pay. She always tried to save up a little extra money for such things, but it wasn't easy. Having Jonathan as a renter for a while would help. Having a doctor in the house might just come in handy, too, she mused, remembering how he'd been so kind when he'd stitched up Julie's head.

Speaking of her handy renter, where was he? She looked out to the spot where he kept his car parked in the back driveway and saw it wasn't there. Where had he gone this early in the day?

Not waiting around, Arabella cleaned the kitchen, got out the supplies to make pies and hummed to herself for the next few minutes. Then she heard a motor purring outside the kitchen window. Jonathan was back. Her heart shouldn't race at that, but she had no way of controlling her erratic heartbeat.

Checking the coffeepot, she was glad she'd just made a fresh pot. She liked having a quiet cup of coffee after the girls were in preschool because her first cup of the morning usually grew cold before she could finish it.

Turning back to her task, Arabella pretended she wasn't curious about where he'd been.

"Do I smell coffee?" he said the minute he closed the back door.

She turned with a smile and immediately noticed how tired he looked. "Yes, I have coffee. And you sure look like you could use a cup. And I have some leftover bread pudding. It's good for breakfast, too." When he didn't immediately respond, she asked, "Are you okay?"

He nodded then slumped against the counter. "I've been with one of your church members."

"Really? Who?" She handed him his coffee then got out the dish of bread pudding from the refrigerator and heated it in the microwave.

"Sara Griffin."

Arabella let out a breath. "She's expecting and having a hard time. I thought she was on bed rest."

"She was," he said, taking a long drink of the coffee, his appreciative gaze on the pudding. "Reverend West called me on my cell at three this morning. She'd gone into labor and she didn't think she'd make it to the hospital. She called him, begging him to call the new doctor in town." He shrugged. "And that would be me."

"You delivered Sara's baby?"

His smiled was etched with fatigue but his expression softened. "I sure did. A boy." He dug into the bread pudding with gusto.

Seeing the pride in his eyes, Arabella reached out a hand to his, patting him on the knuckles. "Jonathan, that's amazing. Thank goodness you were here."

He looked down at her hand over his. "It was pretty remarkable. I've never delivered a baby. So I had to refer back to medical-school training. Makes you stop and think about how important life is, that's for sure."

"I'm sure Sara and her husband appreciated what you did."

"They kept thanking me," he replied before digging for more of the chunky apples and raisins mixed in with the soft bread. "They offered to pay me in installments. I told them not to worry about it. But her husband, Mark, told me I had a free oil change and tire rotation at his shop anytime I want it. And I'm pretty sure he meant that for a lifetime."

"He's the best mechanic around. You'd better take him up on that."

"I will, just to appease his pride if nothing else. I couldn't take the man's money."

Seeing a new side to him, Arabella said, "Doctors have to make a living, same as anyone else."

"But...I'm not officially on duty here, Arabella. I'm a surgeon. I don't do general practice."

"Well, you did today, whether you wanted to or not."

"I guess I did. Darlene Perry and now this. I have to be careful or everyone in town will be calling me."

He was right. Jonathan's cell rang several times over the next few hours.

"Yes, ma'am, I am a doctor. Yes, ma'am, I know all about arthritis pain. Yes, I love steak. But you don't have to pay me with two filets."

"It sounds as if you've just got a bad cold, Mr. Kinnard. I suggest you make a pot of chicken soup and drink plenty of fluids. And get some fresh air. No, sir, you don't have to pay me right away. Just get well soon."

"Dorothy? Is that you?"

"It sure is me, Doc. I hear you've moved into Clayton House. Didn't even know I had competition with Arabella." She chortled. "Lost me a good boarder but I reckon she's a mite bit prettier than I am. Oh, by the way, my left big toe hurts to beat the band. I think I have gout."

So now he was on his way to see Dorothy Henry at the Lucky Lady Inn. She'd offered him eggplants and sweet potatoes from her fall garden in payment.

So this was what it was like being a country doctor?

Only, Jonathan reminded himself, he wasn't a country doctor.

But…he really didn't know who he was anymore.

He pulled up in front of the gaudy green hotel, remembering the first day he'd rolled into town in search of his niece. Looking back now he could see he'd grabbed at this excuse to get away from the stress of his job and a chief of staff who had some control issues. But that excuse had now become an important mission for Jonathan. Even though he probably wouldn't get rich taking care of patients in a general practice, he enjoyed meeting and talking to the gentle, caring people of this town.

Growing up he'd never been a part of any close-knit groups. His mother died when he was five and his daddy never mentioned church, except to tell the boys not to open the front door to "those holier-than-thou, do-gooder busybodies."

Maybe church folks weren't exactly the way his father had led him to believe they were. Maybe some small towns weren't as sad and lonely as the one where he grew up. Or maybe a person could be sad and lonely no matter where he lived or worked.

Unless he knew some caring churchgoers. Unless he knew a cook who made the best apple-and-raisin bread pudding in the world. He had a new favorite guilty pleasure. The pudding and the cook.

He got out of his car, glanced around the quiet streets and smelled the scents of fresh air mixed with old earth and charbroiled meat from the diner. A crisp chill rose over the town green, misty and curling into a light fog from the evaporating dew. But the morning sun chased at that mist, golden rays burning through puffy white clouds with laser precision.

Not bad. Not bad at all.

He went in to visit with Dorothy, determined to do his job to the best of his ability and then decide what to do with the rest of his life. He only had a few more days here so he couldn't offer anyone long-term treatment. He couldn't make a permanent commitment. He'd have to suggest they go to their regular doctors, no matter how far they had to drive.

He tried not to think about Arabella. He didn't want to think about that big old creaking house and the sound of giggles and tiny feet treading down the stairs. He'd be glad to see the last of messy peanut-butter-and-jelly sandwiches and sweet-smelling baby lotion. And although he was steady as a surgeon, he had yet to master puncturing one of those strange juice pouches with a tiny straw. Who thought up this stuff anyway?

When he emerged from the Lucky Lady Inn an hour later, carrying a basket of vegetables to give to Arabella, he saw the good reverend sitting on the big bench near the park. Now what?

"Just the man I want to talk to," Reverend West said, jovial as ever. "I hear you've been treating patients left and right."

"Good morning," Jonathan said, grinning through his greeting. "I've advised a few people, yes. And thanks so much for giving out my cell number."

The minister took Jonathan's sarcasm in stride. "Well, *I* sure couldn't tell any of 'em what to do about their bursitis and bunions, now could I?"

"I guess not." Jonathan sat down on the bench. "I am worried about Darlene, though. She's so frail. From what she's told me regarding her treatment, her kidneys are beginning to fail. She might have to go on dialysis next. She mentioned she's had several seizures—a sure sign that her illness is progressing. She shouldn't be driving, but she said she still gets out now and then. I can't do much for her, I'm afraid. If I could get her to go to Denver for treatment—"

"Just taking time with her helps," the minister answered. "She won't go for treatment. She's made her peace with that. But she told me all about you.

How nice you were and how considerate. Said you even gave Macy a quick physical exam."

"Sweet little girl." He almost asked the minister about that one dimple but decided that might sound like gossip. He wouldn't gossip about a patient. "She seems healthy from what I could tell."

"That's good, son. Real good. You might consider staying on here and becoming our town doctor. Last one left about five years ago. It's a long drive down the interstate to the regional hospital and medical complex." He wiped at his moist brow in spite of the cool temperature. "I can't lie—it's a tough job. All kinds of hours and pretty much any kind of illness, as you saw this morning."

"Yes, sir. I'm used to that, though." Jonathan was about to explain how he couldn't possibly stay on here, but Reverend West was revving up for more. Jonathan figured the man's sermons must be awe-inspiring. He hadn't paid much attention to the one he'd attended because all of his attention had been on Arabella.

"Several of our older homes on Morning Dove Road have been zoned commercial. Any one of 'em would make a fine doctor's office and clinic."

Jonathan had to admire the preacher's boldness. "And you're telling me this because…"

"You know why," the minister replied, his expression dead serious. "Look, son, we need a good doctor. Now I know you're a big-city big shot and all that, but God is the boss. And the Lord brought you here for a reason. You found family here. And you might have found a home."

"What if I don't want a home here?"

"What if you do want a home here?"

Jonathan looked down at the basket of vegetables by his feet. Growing up he'd never had fresh vegetables. He'd rarely had a home-cooked meal. His brother had turned to drink; Jonathan had turned away. He'd never had any desire to settle down in a run-down, closed-down ghost town.

But he'd always had a desire for a family. A real solid, laughing, crying, loving, caring, chaotic, colorful family.

He thought of Arabella again.

And wished he hadn't.

"I can't stay here, Reverend West," he said. "I'm sorry, I just can't." Then he got up and walked back to his car.

"Think about it," Reverend West called. "Pray about it, too."

Jonathan waved a hand but didn't look back. Pray about it? That would be a new one for him. Going to church with Jasmine just so he could sit near Arabella was one thing. But actually praying for peace and the answers to his future?

That was another thing entirely.

Was he ready for that next step?

Jonathan looked down at the fresh vegetables and smiled.

In a town like Clayton, he'd have to be ready for whatever came next.

Even if that meant turning back to God.

Chapter Thirteen

⌒

Arabella dropped her tote bag full of groceries onto the kitchen counter. "Hello, anybody here?"

Her mother's car wasn't parked in the driveway and Jasmine was still at work at the hair salon. Glancing at the clock, she noted it was half past noon. Kat should have brought the girls home by now.

"Do not panic," Arabella told herself, saying the words out loud to reassure her tapping pulse. Maybe Kat stopped for ice cream or decided to take the girls for a stroll in the park. But neither of those things were a priority on Kat's "being a grandmother" list.

"But she does have a cell phone," Arabella said, the echo of her fear hitting the kitchen ceiling. "Kat, call me."

Better yet, Arabella dialed her mother's number, not caring if she was being pesky or not.

"Hey, honey. We're on our way."

Relief washed over Arabella like rain hitting a dry desert.

"Okay, Mama. I'm starting lunch right now."

"Good. The girls said you make the 'bestest' grilled cheese sandwiches."

Arabella tamped down her doubts and concern. "Do you want one?"

"No. I had a bite before I picked up the girls."

Arabella hung up, wondering who her mother had been with this morning. A new boyfriend? An old school friend? Charley or Pauley?

I can't keep my head buried in the sand, she told herself. Her mother was up to something and Arabella wanted to find out about that something, only she didn't have time to go spying on her mother. She'd have to work up the nerve to have a talk with Kat even if she did want to avoid a confrontation.

The door opened and Jasmine hurried in. "I think it's gonna rain. It's cold out there. I have thirty minutes to grab lunch. And that walk made me hungry."

"And hello to you, too," Arabella replied.

"Hey." Jasmine gave her a quick hug. "I love working at the hair salon. I have a view of Eagle Street so I see a lot that goes on in this town."

"Aren't you supposed to be working instead of spying?"

"Oh, I do work. I just watch the window while I do. It's fun."

"And what did you see today?"

Jasmine grabbed a glass and filled it with orange juice. "I saw my handsome uncle cruising by in that fancy silver convertible. Hope he puts the top up before it rains."

Arabella smiled at that. "He was going to see Dorothy Henry. And he probably cut through there to see where you'd be working."

Jasmine tilted her head. "Ah, that's so sweet. But I hear he's doctoring up everybody around here. Did you know he delivered Sara Griffin's baby this morning?"

"He told me. He was mighty proud, too."

Jasmine took a sip of her drink. "I haven't spent much time with him." She grabbed a bag of pretzels. "But he told me we'll go visit my daddy's grave together...maybe this week."

Arabella saw the hesitancy in the girl's eyes. "Do you want to spend time with him?"

"Yes, but I'm not sure how to go about doing that. He's so smart and so different from my daddy. I don't know how to talk to him. We don't have a whole lot in common."

"Oh, honey, just be yourself," Arabella replied. "You're smart, too. You made straight As in high school."

"But...he's a doctor. And Cade wants to be a doctor, so they at least have that to talk about. Cade's in awe of Uncle Jonathan. And I guess I am, too." She chewed her bottom lip. "What if...I can't live up to all this doctor stuff? I'm not even sure I'm cut out to be a doctor's wife."

Arabella came around the counter and took Jasmine by the shoulders. "Has someone been putting this nonsense in your head?"

Jasmine lowered her gaze. "I heard things...at the hair salon. Your cousin Marsha was there. She comes in a lot. Your mother—"

The sound of the door opening caused Jasmine to yank herself away. "It's nothing. I don't think she likes me very much, is all. She's made some mean comments."

"We'll discuss this later," Arabella said, anger boiling over right along with the vegetable soup she was heating for lunch.

Arabella could handle anything Katrina tried to dish out, except her mother being cruel and catty to one of her children. And Jasmine was as much a part of her family as her own three. She wouldn't let her coldhearted mother undermine Jasmine's happiness—no matter what.

Jonathan didn't know why he was driving up Morning Dove Road, except that the name of this particular street was intriguing and not because the very persuasive Reverend West had scouted it out for him. He'd already told Reverend West he couldn't stay here and open a clinic. The logistics of doing that overwhelmed him about as much as being an uncle and meeting a woman with three little girls.

He came here with one purpose in mind—to meet his niece and establish a relationship with her. He'd done that now.

He needed to go back to Denver in a few days, with the hope that Jasmine and Cade would come and visit him at least. Or maybe they'd decide to move to Denver and live near him or with him for a while. He'd really enjoy having them nearby. He'd been dedicated to his work mainly because he didn't have anyone to go home to at the end of the day. Now that could change. He'd still do his job but with a keen eye toward family.

So why was he looking at property for sale in Clayton?

He pulled up to a white cottage-style house that had a big for-sale sign in front. The sign said this property had been zoned for commercial use. Jonathan sat there in the cracked driveway, seeing past the dead limbs and broken windows of the old two-story house, wondering about the family that had lived here. He imagined a tire swing underneath the towering oak and potted flowers sitting on the big porch. Women loved potted flowers, didn't they?

But this house was past its prime, turned commercial to hopefully promote business on this quiet thoroughfare. If someone took this big house and updated it, it would make a nice office for a doctor or a lawyer or any type of business.

Maybe someone would do that one day. But not him. Not now. He quickly backed out of the driveway and headed to Darlene's house out from town. He'd told her he'd stop by again today.

The blue farmhouse looked clean and tidy, making Jonathan wonder if Darlene had help from the church with the upkeep. She'd mentioned how Clayton Community Church had come to her rescue more than once.

Jonathan knocked on the door then glanced at the surrounding countryside. This sure seemed an isolated place to raise a child. Maybe Darlene preferred it that way because she was so sick. And because she didn't like to talk about Macy's daddy.

The door swung open and Darlene stood holding on to it, her eyes as flat and fallow as the field across the road. "Hello, Doc." She pushed at her thinning dark blond hair. "C'mon in."

Jonathan dreaded going into the dainty living room. Darlene kept it neat and tidy but the aura of sickness and death seemed to permeate the very walls, bringing back long-held memories of when his mother had been so sick. A white chenille throw lay on the gray couch and a scrawny plant sat in the middle of a battered coffee table along with a tray full of prescription drugs. A small television mounted to the wall over the fireplace droned on and on, the twenty-four-hour news station reporting on world events.

Jonathan waited for Darlene to sit down on the couch, then he lowered himself into a puffy blue rocking chair/recliner next to the sofa. "How are you today, Darlene?"

"I had a rough night," she said, her gray eyes washed out. "A lot of pain. My skin itches so badly."

Jonathan glanced at the medicine bottles. "Are you tolerating the steroids?"

Darlene made a face. "Tolerating? That's a good word for it. Between the steroids and the pain pills, I guess I'm tolerating things pretty well. My regular doc told me I might have to take some morphine shots if it gets worse. And don't even get me started on where my kidneys are going."

Jonathan nodded. "I've done some research online about lupus since I last saw you. Sometimes lupus can be controlled and overcome, but you're in the advanced stages of the disease. It might help if you could eat a healthy, balanced diet and get outside more to exercise."

"Doc, I can't make it past the few steps to the door most days. I'm not even supposed to drive, but I can get around town when I have to." She waved a boney hand toward the kitchen. "People from the church take turns bringing me food and…sometimes running errands and helping with Macy."

Jonathan saw the embarrassment in her eyes.

"That's good. I'm glad you have your church to turn to."

"I didn't always," she said, lowering her eyes. Staring down at her hands, she went on. "I...did some things I'm not proud of. I was young and gullible. But I have Macy now and she's such a blessing. That's why it's important to me to make sure she has people to watch over her if...after I'm gone."

"What about her father?" Jonathan asked, remembering Macy's cute dimple. Maybe Darlene would open up about that subject today.

Darlene glanced away. "Like I told you before, he's out of the picture. End of discussion."

"But couldn't he help with your situation?"

Darlene sat back against the old couch then pulled a pink shawl around her shoulders. "Macy's father gave me money long ago. I bought this house, put part of the money up for her college education and put the rest in savings. But with me being sick...I went through my savings pretty quickly. I won't touch the money I put away for Macy." She shrugged. "Besides, it's too late to ask her father for help. Way too late."

Jonathan didn't like being nosy, but he had to ask, "Does she know about him?"

"No, not really. He couldn't be a father to her so we parted ways even before she was born. After I found out about the lupus, I turned to God for help. Back when I was pregnant and unmarried I promised Macy's father I wouldn't make trouble for him. You see, he was already married and had his own family. He promised to help us financially and he did set up an account almost immediately, but then he died before I had my baby."

Shock hit Jonathan in the gut while Darlene's expression clouded over with grief. "That's terrible. I'm so sorry."

"Yes, I am, too. But I've kept my promise. I haven't revealed his identity to anyone. And I won't." She glanced out the window. "No matter who thinks I need to tell the truth."

Wondering if someone was pressuring her, Jonathan patted her hand. "How can you keep that kind of promise?"

"I promised God," Darlene said, her words quiet. "I did a bad thing, messing with a married man. But I didn't want my child to suffer because of that. So I turned to God and I promised Him if he'd help my Macy, I'd be the best mother possible while I'm still around and I'd let the past stay in the past. As far as Macy knows, her father died. That's the truth. That's all she needs to know."

Jonathan wondered at that. Surely the child would question who her father really was. But he had to admire Darlene's strong convictions. She'd suffered to protect her child and the family of the man who'd fathered Macy. And she'd done it because she'd promised God she'd try to be a better person. Things could have turned out a lot worse all the way around if she had revealed the father. A lot of people would have been hurt. It took a certain amount of courage and sacrifice to make that kind of decision.

He checked Darlene's vitals then sat back in his chair. "I can't do a whole lot for you, Darlene. I've called a colleague in Denver who specializes in this type of disease to see if he has any suggestions, but other than that I can only monitor you and try to make you comfortable." He looked her square in the eyes. "And I can listen. I'm good at listening."

"You've gone beyond the call of duty, Doc," she said with a soft smile. "I'm okay. I've made my peace with the Lord and I've found some good folks to look after Macy. Like you said, there's not much anyone can do for me. I've done my best to make amends for my bad decisions." She gave him a long stare. "I can give you some advice, though. You came here to find family and I think that's a fine thing. Make the most of it, Doc. You only get a few second chances in life. I say take advantage of what the good Lord's put in front of you…before it's too late."

Jonathan couldn't argue with that gentle suggestion. "I wish I'd had that chance with my brother."

"You're here now," Darlene said. "You have a chance with his daughter. And that girl needs you."

"I'll try and do right by her." Darlene was wise,

of course. But Jonathan didn't want to break down and reveal all his woes and fears. He checked his watch and made a big production of getting his medical bag together. "Well, I'll be in town for a few more days. I'll check back with you before I leave. Call me if you need anything before then."

Darlene tried to stand but Jonathan helped her back down. "Can I get you anything before I leave?"

"I'm fine for now," Darlene said. "A friend is bringing lunch."

He nodded and left, shutting the door behind him. The wind picked up, indicating that the dark clouds brewing over the horizon were about to rain down on the countryside. Then he glanced down at a bad spot in the porch where several boards were broken and rotten. Jonathan knew how to use a hammer and nails. He could probably fix this porch. And the sooner he did, the better because he didn't want Darlene or Macy falling through those loose boards. Deciding he'd do that, he also figured he could ask Cade to help him. It was time he got to know Cade a little better anyway.

Rain fell in heavy gray sheets as the afternoon progressed.

Arabella had six loaves of bread cooling on the counter and she'd baked three pies—sweet potato, apple and rhubarb—for the Cowboy Café. Tomorrow, she'd bake the tiers for the Burfords' anniversary cake, then she'd ice them first thing Friday morning.

Glancing at the clock, she figured she had about twenty more minutes of quiet time before the triplets woke up from their nap. She loved it when the house was quiet like this. Her mother was up in her room, probably taking her own nap or working on whatever shifty things she had going and Jasmine was home from work and putting away clean clothes.

They hadn't been able to continue their conversation regarding Katrina, nor had Arabella found a chance to talk to her mother. She'd get to the bottom of whatever Kat had said to upset Jasmine before the day was over.

But where in the world was the handsome Dr. Turner?

And why in the world did she care?

She heard a motor purring and glanced out the back window. Wow, just thinking about the man had brought him home.

Home? The man was renting a room.

"Get over it," Arabella said in a tight whisper, wishing she didn't get all fluttery whenever Jonathan was around. It didn't make a bit of sense, this shaky, light feeling that rushed over her when he entered the room.

"Hey," he said, smiling as he shook drops of

water off his coat. "I tried to drip out on the porch, but I think some of the rain stayed on me."

"It's okay," she said, throwing him a clean towel. "These floors can handle just about anything."

"If walls could talk." His gaze moved around the room. "I just left Darlene. She knows she's dying, and yet, she's willing to protect Macy's unknown father. Amazing."

"We've all wondered about that," Arabella replied, seeing the dark confusion in his eyes. "How is she?"

"Not good." He put his elbows on the counter. "Those pies look great, though."

"I have extra in the oven."

He grinned at that but then went blank, his expression turning thoughtful. "Have you ever been around Darlene's daughter, Macy?"

"A few times here and there. She's a pretty little girl. Very shy."

"Yes. She has the cutest dimple right here." He reached out and touched Arabella's cheek. "It reminds me of you. Your girls have that same dimple."

Arabella pulled away, surprised. "What are you suggesting, Jonathan?"

"I don't know," he said with a shrug. "It's just when you put things together—it makes you wonder. Darlene is dying now and she's suddenly pushing her daughter toward your family. Why?"

Arabella crossed her arms and held them tightly to her body. "And Macy has a dimple on one cheek same as my cousins and me."

"Yes."

"Not to mention that the girl has blond hair and blue eyes, too."

"That's right—"

"You know something, Jonathan? You can't just come to town and start speculating about people. If you have something to say, just say it."

He leaned into the counter. "Okay. I think Macy could possibly be the daughter of one of your dead uncles."

Arabella's pulse shot up and danced across her system. She wished she'd never mentioned her uncles to him. "That's ridiculous! I feel for Darlene but I can assure you Macy is not a Clayton. Both of my uncles were happily married men."

"And Darlene said the father was married. That's why she never revealed his name. She didn't want to hurt his family. Or Macy." He leaned against the counter, his expression imploring. "I may be out of line here, but this situation is urgent. That woman is dying and her daughter will believe she's all alone. We both know how that feels, Arabella. I had to ask because I trust you. And…I thought you'd want to know, just in case."

The logical part of Arabella's brain told her what

Jonathan was suggesting made sense. But the emotional part couldn't accept that theory.

"My cousins have been through a lot," she said, lowering her voice. "They all lost their fathers on the same day. I think that's why they left, one by one. They couldn't deal with the pain and the grief. You can't spread this around, not now when each one of them is coming back to honor my grandfather's will. You don't have that right, do you understand?"

"I understand," Jonathan said, coming around the counter to face her. "I only told you, in confidence, because I'm concerned about Macy. If Brooke and Zach have already bonded with her, then maybe Darlene is doing the right thing. It's something to think about."

"Just keep it to yourself," Arabella said, shaking her head. "I have to go and check on the girls."

She rushed out of the room, leaving him standing there in the kitchen. But when she reached the stairs, she stopped and held a hand to her chest. Jonathan was a smart man and his sense of logic was very clear. He wouldn't speculate on this if he didn't believe he had stumbled onto the truth.

And what if he was right?

Chapter Fourteen

The rain came down in shimmering sheets that caused rivulets of water to stream onto the street. The leaves on the trees, already loosened from the change of the seasons, fell into the rain and then lay limp and wet against the mushy grass. A gray, dreary dusk hung over the houses and streets and the distant mountains turned from gray stone to mauve hulking shadows. The old-fashioned gas lamp streetlights sent an eerie yellow glow out onto the quiet street.

Jonathan turned from the big bay window in the parlor. "I hope Jasmine drives carefully. It's a bad night to be out gallivanting around."

"She's a responsible driver," Arabella said, looking up from the book she was reading to Jamie. "Her friend doesn't live too far away."

Jessie came up to Jonathan, tugging on his shirt sleeve. "Play Chutes and Ladders with me, please?"

"It's been ages since I played. You'll have to show me how."

"Okay." Jessie ran to a shelf in the corner and produced the board game. "C'mon, Julie."

Arabella spoke up. "You'll need to help them count. We use that game to teach them to count to one hundred."

"I think I can count that high," Jonathan replied with a smile. He glanced over the board and figured out how to spin the wheel and count out the number of steps indicated by whatever the wheel stopped on. The goal was to get across the board without going down too many chutes. He had a goal of his own—to get back in the good graces of his landlord.

Hoping to test the waters with Arabella after their earlier discussion about Darlene and Macy, Jonathan had entertained the girls and helped with dinner. She'd been civil enough during the meal, but he could tell she had a lot on her mind. Katrina and Jasmine had kept the table discussions going, but Arabella hadn't contributed much to the conversation. He didn't need to add to her worries by suggesting one of her uncle's might have fathered Macy Perry. But his gut told him that had to be the case. From all the hints Darlene had dropped, and the way she'd suddenly starting pushing her daughter toward Arabella's cousins Zach and Brooke, it all added up. But it wasn't his business. He'd have to learn to keep his conclusions to himself.

"Let me get this fire going, Jessie," he said now. "I think this storm is going to hang around the rest of the night."

Arabella glanced outside. "You could be right about that. It'll be cooler tomorrow, too. I'll make white chili for dinner with corn bread."

Jonathan smiled then plopped down to continue the game. After Jessie had carefully and methodically explained how it worked, they went into action. It looked as if Jessie might just beat her sister and him. Watching as Julie took her turn spinning the wheel to see how far she could get up the path, he glanced over at Arabella. "Do you know how often you mention food in any conversation?"

Arabella turned the page of the picture book and waited for Jamie to repeat the word to her. "Cat. That's right. *C-A-T.* Cat. Very good, Jamie." After they finished the book, Jamie got out of her lap and ran to play with a miniature dollhouse.

"I'm sorry," Arabella said to Jonathan. "I guess I have food on my mind a lot. I am the chief cook and bottle washer around here and I do make my living baking and cooking."

"Well, I'm not complaining," he replied, enjoying the slight blush on her cheeks while he tried to clarify his words. "I like it. I mean, your cooking is great."

Could he be any worse at trying to get closer to this woman? He was definitely playing a game here and he was losing, big-time, no matter how he tried to put a spin on things. He didn't need any chute to go down, but he could use a ladder to get himself out of this hole he'd managed to dig.

"I guess you do. You sure eat enough of my food."

"I'll help with the groceries," he retorted, knowing she'd turn him down as she always did. Her mood didn't seem to be improving with this conversation, either.

"I charge you room and board and that includes meals." Her smile belied the seriousness of her words. "I enjoy cooking."

"And I'm a lucky man for that." He finished the game, conceding to Jessie's superiority and deciding she definitely took after her mother. The girls cleared away the game and went to harass their sister.

Jonathan got up, groaning. "I'm getting too old to sit cross-legged on the floor."

"Better do more stretches. We have a lot of on-the-floor playtime around here."

"So I'm learning." He sank down across from Arabella, thinking that in spite of her snippy comments tonight, a man could get used to this. Even just sitting still, she managed to keep working. She liked to knit.

And he liked to watch her knit.

Arabella knitted with the same intensity as when she baked bread and cakes or cared for her children. Her forehead furrowed into a cute, focused expression. Her pretty, pouty lips pursed up into that determined way he'd also noticed in her children's expressions. She was the real deal, a true earth mother and nurturer and completely protective of her family. Even the family members who treated her so badly. And she wasn't going to take any bunk from him apparently.

He'd never known anyone like Arabella. It occurred to him that he'd been spending more time with her than he had with his niece. Maybe he should work on that so Jasmine wouldn't misinterpret his reasons for hanging around. But he couldn't deny Arabella was one of those reasons.

"Why are you staring at me?" she asked, stopping her needles to look at him.

"Am I staring? Sorry." He smiled at her then shrugged. "When I first heard about Jasmine, I almost didn't come here. I was afraid she'd turn me away. But I never dreamed I'd be welcomed into your home and…that I'd be able to get to know not only my niece, but also her family."

Arabella dropped her knitting. "We are her family. I'm glad you can see that."

"Of course I can. And I don't want that to change." He inhaled deeply. "Except to let me be a part of it, too."

She lifted her chin. "You want to be a part of my family?"

The question was asked with awe and a tad of doubt.

"Does that bother you?"

She gave him a look that held conflicting emotions, part grimace and part grin. "I haven't decided yet. But if you keep being nosy regarding my blood relatives, you might not make the cut."

Letting out a sigh, he put his hands on his jeans. "You're right. It's not my place to make observations about people I don't even know. Won't happen again."

"Good. Because I can't deal with rumors about Darlene Perry right now. I have enough on my plate." She cringed. "Oops, there I go interjecting something about food again."

"Okay, I get it," Jonathan said, wishing he'd gone to bed early the way Kitty Kat had. "I'll stay out of your business from now on."

He wanted to say more, but the front door burst open and Jasmine came in, tugging off her scarf and raincoat.

"It's raining cats and dogs out there," she said, tossing her damp hair over her shoulders.

Jessie got up and ran to the window. "I don't see any cats, Jasmine. No dogs out there, either."

Jasmine grabbed the little girl and gave her a big kiss. "I was just teasing. It's mostly raining water."

"I wanted to see the cats," Jessie said, making a face.

Jasmine put her down with a laugh, then glanced at Arabella. "I want to try on my dress again and send Mariette a picture. And we can take a picture of the material we found for the bridesmaid dresses. She'll be one of my attendants and I want her to see it."

Arabella put away her knitting basket. "That's fine. We'll take pictures and email them to her."

Jasmine grinned at Jonathan. "Mariette is my best friend, but she's away at college. I've told her all about you, though."

"Really now?" Jonathan wondered what she'd said about him.

"It's all good," Jasmine said. "Besides, we both love your car." Then she changed the subject back to the wedding. "I can't wait for you to see what Arabella will be wearing in the wedding."

Jonathan looked down at Arabella. "You're in the wedding?"

"Maid of honor," she replied with a twist of a smile. "I tried to talk her out of that notion, but she insisted."

He nodded his approval. "I think that's nice. And you deserve a place of honor."

"Stop trying to butter me up." She stood and started picking up toys, her efficiency drowning out any praise he might offer. "Bedtime, girls." Then she turned back to Jonathan. "I want that girl to be happy. I'm praying toward that end. So if that means I have to put on a fancy dress and stand with her when she takes her vows, then so be it."

While the girls picked up toys, Jonathan drew closer to Arabella. "Listen, I'm sorry for my assumptions earlier, okay? I have no right to even suggest anything about Macy's parentage. So can we just get past my blunder?"

She faced him, her eyes clear and without rancor. "It's all right. I'm sure you didn't say anything that hasn't been whispered around here before. My own mother's hinted at the same but I tend to ignore her observations." She looked into his eyes. "But the thing is, now that *you've* mentioned Darlene and Macy, I can't get that out of my mind. Several people have said the same thing recently. It's just one more secret coming to light. I don't want to believe it, Jonathan."

"I know you don't and I could be wrong. We could all be wrong. Let's just forget I said anything. I'm a doctor—not some armchair commentator. It's not like me to deal in gossip or speculations. I usually go on concrete facts."

Arabella gazed up at him, her eyes full of understanding and worry. "It's okay. Everyone around here is a commentator on one thing or another. That's small-town life for you."

"One of the reasons I left the town where I grew up," he replied. "My family certainly suffered the brunt of gossip and talk."

"Then you know how it feels." The expression on her face changed to one of regret, making him wish he hadn't said anything about his own past.

Arabella loved her home and this town. Her ancestors had built Clayton. She had a vested interest in keeping the place alive and thriving because she had a deep-rooted connection here.

He'd never had that kind of connection to any place.

But standing here with her, he wished he'd find a place, a home that grounded him rather than disgraced him. He lived in Denver, but he didn't really have a life there. Arabella had a life, a real honest-to-goodness life, with all the good and bad and the ups and downs that came with it.

"Let's just forget I ever mentioned it," he said.

They stood there staring at each other, so close that Jonathan could easily reach and kiss her. *Easily.* But before he knew what was happening, the girls were gathered around them singing "Ring Around the Roses."

Their shrill chant broke the tension and caused

Arabella to try and move away. "Okay, enough. Bedtime," she said, her words breathless, her gaze locked on Jonathan.

But the girls kept chanting and giggling as they got closer and closer, and that forced her closer toward Jonathan. He didn't mind. Not one bit. He liked the fresh scent of her hair, the freckles sprinkled across her nose, the tilt of her proud chin.

He shifted and tried to steady himself but when he practically fell into her arms, Arabella held her hands up against his chest then looked straight into his eyes.

And that's how they wound up together, a breath away, her eyes bright with expectation and his heart pumping with newfound adrenaline.

"I need to—"

"We should—"

Arabella pulled away. "Girls, stop it now. Upstairs for baths. Find your jammies and put them on your beds. I'll be right there."

She watched as they ran toward the stairs, their little feet hitting the hardwood floor with a delicate melody of pitter-pattering.

"I have to go," she said, turning to Jonathan with a confused smile.

He held her arm. "I understand." But he didn't understand what was happening to him. "Arabella, we need to talk."

"The girls, Jonathan. I can't leave them alone. I'll be back in a few minutes. You're welcome to wait."

He would wait because he certainly wouldn't be able to sleep until they'd talked. But what would he say to her? *Hey, I'm attracted to you and I'd like to kiss you, but I can't stay here...and you need more than I can offer.* Yeah, that'd go over well.

He busied himself with making notes on the patients he'd talked to over the past few days, jotting things down in the pocket notebook he kept handy and backing it up with his smartphone notes. A couple of them needed follow-up visits. Especially Darlene.

She had taught Jonathan something that working in a big hospital never had. Sometimes a sick person just needed to sit and talk. And as a doctor, *he* needed to listen. He'd told her he was a good listener, but that wasn't really true. He listened to symptoms and made diagnoses but he'd never before actually listened to the underlying currents of a patient's fears and concerns. But with Darlene he'd had no other choice. He couldn't make her well.

Maybe that's why he'd noticed things, been more observant and alert with her. He'd seen the resemblance to the Claytons in Macy from the start. Was he wrong?

He was learning to listen with his heart and diagnose with his head. Over the past few days, he'd added another important component to his skills. Prayer. Maybe prayer would help him through his feelings for Arabella, too.

Starting right now. "Lord, I need some guidance."

He heard Arabella coming back down the stairs and smiled up at her as she entered the parlor. "I picked up the rest of the toys."

She looked around, her hands on her hips. "Thanks."

Jonathan swallowed, gathered his thoughts then started toward her. "Arabella—"

Jasmine came running into the room. "I can't find my dress, Arabella. Did you take it out of my closet?"

Arabella pulled away, almost stumbling over the toy basket. "My mom put it in the hall closet last time I was working on it, honey."

Jasmine pivoted toward the hallway then banged the closet door open. "I don't see it."

Arabella went to search the closet. "That's odd. I know she put it in here. I saw her. I told her to put it here instead of in your room, so she wouldn't wake you."

"Can I ask her?" Jasmine started up the stairs.

"I think she's asleep," Arabella called. "Check in your closet again."

Jasmine turned at the top of the stairs to stare down at Arabella and Jonathan, her hands flailing in the air. "I've checked there several times. It's not there. Can I check in your room?"

Arabella nodded. "Sure, but I doubt it's in my closet."

Wanting to help, Jonathan said, "I'll check the laundry room and the closet in my room. Maybe Katrina moved it again without telling you."

He shot Arabella a worried look and saw his feelings mirrored on her face. Then he hurried to the back of the house and went through every closet in his room and the laundry room.

The dress wasn't anywhere to be found.

"I'm going to wake my mother," Arabella said when he came back. "She might remember where she put it." But she stopped and leaned close to Jonathan before she went upstairs. "Jonathan, I saw her put it in that closet. What could have happened?"

Jonathan couldn't answer that. "We'll find the dress. You go talk to your mother and I'll go check on the girls."

"They should be asleep, but the way Jasmine's running around this house, she might get them wound up again."

"I'll try to calm her down, too." He guided Arabella up the stairs, stopping at the turret window on the landing to let her go ahead of him.

And that's when he saw it in the dim glow of the backyard security light. Just a glance at first, but then a trail of white floating in the rain and the wind.

Jasmine's wedding dress was hanging on a tree in the backyard.

Chapter Fifteen

"Arabella, look."

Jonathan pointed to the wisps of white moving in the wind.

Arabella gasped and put a hand to her mouth. "Oh, no. Oh, Jonathan, how did that get out there?"

"Good question." He put his hands on her arms. "I'll go get it. You need to find Jasmine."

"She can't see it," Arabella said. "But...we can't hide it from her, either. She'll be devastated."

"I'll figure something out," he replied. "Get her downstairs so we don't disturb the girls."

Arabella nodded. "I think I'll be sure and wake my mama anyway. She was the last person to have a hand on this dress."

Jonathan didn't like the expression on her face. It didn't bode well for Katrina Watson. But why would her mother do something so vile?

"I'll be right back."

Hurrying down the stairs and toward the back

door, he grabbed a rain slicker he saw on the hall tree. Throwing the slicker over his head, he rushed out into the muddy backyard.

The dress was snagged on a low-hanging branch of a ponderosa pine. Wondering if the dress had been somewhere else and the wind had picked it up and dropped it here, Jonathan reached up to carefully lift the delicate dress off the wet branch. It was heavy with water, so he didn't think the wind could have tossed it. Someone had deliberately left it in plain sight in the backyard. Holding it close, he ran back to the house.

The dress was ruined. Torn and muddy and soggy. He didn't know how anyone could restore it. He stood in the hallway, dripping onto the welcome rug, his heart shredding in the same jagged pattern of the dress. How could he bear to show this to Jasmine?

Too late.

She came barreling around the corner, her eyes wide with shock and disbelief. "What happened?"

Jonathan clung to the dress, watering dripping down into his eyes. "I found it outside, honey. I'm so sorry."

Arabella and Katrina came to stand behind Jasmine. Arabella reached for the girl. "We'll fix it. Somehow, we'll fix it."

Jasmine spun around, tears in her eyes. "How?

How can anyone fix that? Look at it. It's ruined. I don't understand what happened."

Jonathan looked at the women staring over at him. "Somebody deliberately took this dress." He couldn't help but suspect Katrina. From the beginning she'd seemed hostile toward Jasmine. But why?

"Don't look at me," Katrina said, staring him down. Her red hair was spiked and mushed and she wore leopard-print pajamas and a matching robe. Without all her makeup, she looked old and scrawny. "Last time I saw that dress, it was in the hall closet."

"Mom, are you sure you didn't move it?" Arabella asked, her expression daring.

"I told you, I put it right there in the closet just like you told me to do." Looking offended, Katrina held her chin in the air. "Why would I go to the trouble of putting a wedding dress out in the rain?"

Jonathan couldn't be sure about the woman, but she had a point. "That's what I'd like to know. Who would do this and why?"

Jasmine reached for the dress, tears streaming down her face. "Lots of people are trying to stop this wedding. It could have been anybody." She took the wet dress over to the counter then sat down on a high chair, holding it against her. "I loved my dress. I wanted Cade to see me in this dress. Now that can't happen."

Arabella grabbed her cell phone out of her pocket. "I'm calling Zach. He might be able to find some prints or clues or something."

Jasmine kept staring at the ruined dress. "I can't tell Cade about this tonight. He'll storm over here and want to hurt somebody. And right now I would be very ugly toward his family members because I'm pretty sure one of them did this. I'll wait and call him tomorrow."

Arabella put her phone away. "Zach's on his way." Then she went to Jasmine. "Let me have it, baby. I might be able to clean it up and rework it."

But when she turned back around, the dress dragging in her hands, Jonathan saw the dejected look on her face. The torn, muddy mess in her arms couldn't be fixed. The skirt was shredded and the beadwork she'd sewn by hand was ripped away, leaving tiny holes in the once-shiny material. Arabella might not be able to fix this dress, but *he* could sure try and find one to replace it.

And he could certainly try to find the person who did this. Jonathan hadn't come here for a fight, but now he was more than willing to get involved in one.

Zach sat with Arabella the next morning and drank coffee as he tried to help her put the pieces of this puzzle together.

"So you're telling me we might not ever find out

who did this?" Arabella asked, exhaustion from being up so late dragging through her system.

Zach put down his coffee cup. "Yep. It was raining, which washed away what few footprints I might have found. And as for fingerprints, well, this house has a lot of people coming and going. No telling what I'll find on the closet door or on the back door."

Arabella saw the truth in her cousin's eyes. "In other words, this isn't a priority for the sheriff's department?"

"It's not that," Zach replied. "This is serious, but it's vandalism at the most. It'll be hard to prove anything. I'm sorry."

"Yeah, me, too. I'm sorry that Jasmine's pretty dress is beyond repair."

Zach sat up and put his hands on his knees. "What about Kat?"

"What about her? She said she put the dress in the closet and I saw her do it. She's all in a twit because Jonathan looked like he might like her for the crime."

Zach grinned at her police speak. "Like her?"

She slapped at his arm. "You know what I mean. The house was locked all day yesterday. You said yourself, no signs of forced entry anywhere."

"But several people have a key," Zach said. "Including Jasmine and Cade, your mother and… Jonathan Turner."

Arabella shook her head. "Jonathan wouldn't do that to Jasmine. He saw her in the dress. He knew how important this was to her."

"But he has expressed being against the wedding."

"We all have." She shrugged. "And Cade does have a key but he's the groom. He sure wouldn't do anything to sabotage his own wedding. Besides, he was at work all day yesterday."

"Well, that leaves your mother. You said you left the house for a few hours. She could have doubled back after she dropped off the girls."

"I've thought of that," Arabella admitted. "But she had an early lunch with somebody."

"At the Cowboy Café?"

"She didn't say. I think it would have been too risky for her to come back for the dress."

"But you do see that she had an opportunity?"

Arabella got up to put their cups away. "I do see that, yes. But, Zach, even my mother wouldn't stoop that low, would she?"

Zach rubbed a hand over his chin. "We still don't know why she's here. If she's after money from the will, stopping the wedding wouldn't give her that."

Arabella stared out at the tree where they'd found the dress, thinking how different things could look after a storm. "No, it wouldn't. Her only purpose would be to make my life miserable."

"Well, there you go, then."

"It couldn't have been her, Zach. I just can't wrap my brain around that. But the house was locked up and empty for a few hours yesterday. Somebody got to that dress somehow."

Zach leaned over the counter. "There is the whole other Clayton clan to consider. We both know how Pauley and Charley feel about Cade marrying Jasmine. Even Cousin Frank has made several comments about our side of the family. That old feud has been growing strong again since the will was read."

"Yes. Pauley and Charley confronted us in the café the other day, making fun of the wedding and all of us. Cade heard them, too, and told them to back off. And Jonathan stepped in to warn them off."

"We don't need him being a hero now," Zach warned. "Where is he this morning anyway?"

"He took Jasmine to breakfast before she had to go to work. I think they were going to visit Aaron's grave, too. Then he planned to come back here and check on some patients."

"I heard he's become somewhat of a country doctor." Zach grinned then touched a knuckle to her arm. "And apparently he's been seen with you around town a lot."

"He's staying in my house, Zach. Hard to avoid the man."

"You like him, don't you?"

The questioning look on her handsome cousin's face made Arabella blush. "He's a nice man. And a good man. He's been a big help to Jasmine. She needs family now more than ever."

"He and Cade apparently plan to do some repairs at Darlene Perry's house. Your doctor is making a name for himself around here."

"He's not *my* doctor." Arabella thought about Jonathan's theory regarding Macy Perry. But she didn't bring that up to her cousin. "He's a kind person so I'm not surprised he'd offer to help Darlene."

Zach didn't press her. When his cell phone buzzed, Arabella breathed a sigh of relief. She wasn't ready to discuss her feelings for Jonathan. This latest upheaval only added to the pressures in her life. No wonder the man was gun-shy around her and her kids. He didn't want a small-town kind of life and he certainly didn't need any drama like this. So she didn't need to think about how nice it was having him around.

Zach motioned to Arabella. "It's about Lucas. I'll put it on speaker so you can hear, too." He hit a button on his phone and placed it on the counter then whispered, "It's the private investigator."

"Go ahead," he said into the phone.

"Okay, here's the deal," the male voice said. "Seems your cousin stumbled into a dangerous situation. An alleged buddy of his was murdered by some drug lord from what I can glean. And the druggies kidnapped the man's kid—a three-year-old boy. The kid might have witnessed the murder."

Arabella let out a breath. "What about Lucas?"

"A man fitting his description was seen at the junkie's house in the Everglades. But these people aren't stupid. That house is empty. They're probably moving the boy every few days. From everything I've managed to piece together, my bet is that Lucas is trying to rescue that kid."

"Knowing Lucas, I agree," Zach said, his expression grim. "I should alert the locals on this, but that might put Lucas and the boy in danger."

"What do you want me to do?" the man asked.

"Just keep tracking him," Zach replied. "But don't get involved. Lucas is smart. He'll call when he has a chance. Until then, I have to believe he's better off if we don't interfere."

"Are you sure?" Arabella asked, her heart burning with worry for her cousin. "He needs help, Zach."

Zach's brow furrowed into a frown. "It's the best we can do for now. It's too dangerous. Okay, keep us posted." He thanked the man and hung up, his gaze on Arabella. "Lucas knows how to take care of himself."

"But these people will kill him if they find him," Arabella retorted, worry coursing through her. "And the child, too."

"Yes, they could do that. All the more reason

to trust him on this. Lucas won't put himself in danger, and he sure won't do anything to jeopardize that little boy. He'll stay alive until he has that kid back."

She didn't like it, but then she wasn't a cop. "We should call Vivienne and Mei and let them know."

"Yeah and I need to tell Brooke, too," Lucas replied. "Why don't I go do that and you can call the others? Just tell them what we know and why we're staying out of it." He put his hands on his hips. "And I mean that, Arabella. Stress the importance of not interfering. If either of them hears from Lucas, I need to know right away."

"They'll both call you about your decision, you know."

He gave her a quick kiss on the forehead. "That's why I need to get back to the office. I'll be ready for them. I don't like this, either, but…what else can we do from here?"

"Pray," Arabella suggested.

"Always." Zach hurried out the front door.

Moments later, Jonathan came through the back door.

"Hi," he said, smiling over at her. "Baking that big cake?"

She nodded, her worries for Lucas front and center in her mind. "For the Burfords. I'll ice it later and deliver it tomorrow afternoon." She put down her dish towel. "How's Jasmine?"

"She's okay," he said as he headed to the coffee-pot. "Cade met us for breakfast and made her feel better. He offered to go with us to the gravesite, but Jasmine didn't want him to be late for work." He filled his mug and took a long appreciative sip. "I could see how worried he was, though. He didn't say much when she suggested someone close to him might have ruined her wedding gown. But I wonder if he blames his family and he just won't voice it."

"Probably. I can't think who else would be so mean."

"Me, either." He walked to a stool and sat down. "Arabella, I've ordered her a new dress."

"What?"

"I called a friend in Denver and described the dress to her," Jonathan explained. "I hope I got the details right. She went online and found a couple that sounded very similar. She's sent some pictures to my phone and I picked one. It should be delivered in two days."

Arabella was so stunned she didn't know what to say. "How did you know what size?"

"I managed to ask Jasmine when we were eating. I told her maybe she could find something in one of the boutiques or secondhand stores here in town. Anything to make her feel better."

"Did she buy that suggestion?"

"I think so. But she's not in the mood to look yet. She's so down that I wanted to help. So don't say anything, please. Just let me do this. I know it won't be the same, but I…need to do this for my niece." He stared out the window. "She really broke down at the gravesite, but…I think she needed to get it all out of her system. I wasn't so sure we should go there this morning, even though we'd planned our trip before the dress went missing. But we had a good talk on the drive back into town."

Arabella could see the concern in his eyes. "Okay," she finally said. "I won't tell her about the dress." She checked on her cake layers in the oven. Almost done. "That was mighty nice of you, Jonathan. She'll be so touched."

He stared down at the counter. "I wish I could find the person who hung that dress out on that tree. They had to have waited until dark. But before that, someone came into your house."

"It's scary, but Zach says it will be hard to prove. I can't afford security so I guess I'll just have to start with changing the locks."

"You think they had a key?"

She met his eyes. "How else could they get in here?"

"Well, you do have lots of windows and doors around this place."

"That's true." She stared at the back door. "And honestly, sometimes I'm in such a hurry I tend to leave the back door unlocked. I've tried to be more mindful of that since I redid the apartment for renters."

"I always lock it when I leave," he replied.

"And you left before me yesterday."

He quirked a brow. "So I'm off the hook?"

"I never said you were a suspect."

"But you had to think it. I'm sure your deputy-sheriff cousin sure did."

She lifted a shoulder. "Okay, yes, but that's his job. He has to rule out suspects, starting with everyone close to Jasmine."

"Did he rule me out?"

"*I* ruled you out," she retorted. "You wouldn't do that to Jasmine."

"No, I wouldn't." He came over to her and gave her a long glance. "Are you all right?"

"We got some news on my cousin Lucas."

"Oh. Can you talk about it?" he asked.

"I shouldn't but I think I can trust you."

"You know you can trust me," he said.

Arabella poured herself a cup of coffee, took a container of chocolate-chip cookies out of the pantry and sat down beside him. As she offered him some cookies and took one for herself, she realized that she did trust Jonathan. He was becoming a good friend and he was trying to be good to Jasmine.

So she told him what they'd learned from the private investigator. It sure felt good to have someone to talk to about this, someone who wasn't related.

Someone who was becoming more and more important to her.

"Thanks for listening," she said.

Jonathan reached out a hand to cover hers. "I don't mind. I think I've learned to be a better listener since coming here."

Arabella saw the warmth in his eyes and felt her heart grow warmer from his touch. What was happening to her? He must have felt the jolt of awareness, too. He leaned close, his gaze moving over her face, his eyes as gray as the sky had been yesterday, his soft smile as welcoming as the sunshine pushing through the many windows.

The slamming of the front door brought them apart.

Jasmine stomped into the kitchen, her eyes bright with tears. "It's over, Arabella. The wedding is off!"

Chapter Sixteen

"What do you mean?" Arabella asked. "Did Charley say something to you?"

Jasmine threw her purse up on the table. "No, but his son did."

"Oh, no! What did he say?"

Jasmine stood, her shoulders braced, her feet planted wide apart. "Cade came by the shop to see if I wanted to take a quick break. We got into this argument about the wedding dress and he actually defended his father and told me to stop accusing his family."

Arabella gave Jonathan an imploring look.

"What exactly did you say?" Jonathan asked, his tone quiet and calm.

"I told him that his family was dead set against our getting married and he needed to make them understand that we love each other. Then I said I thought one of them had deliberately tried to ruin my dress."

"So he got angry?" Arabella asked.

"Yes and…it seemed like the whole town was listening. I guess I just gave Charley Clayton exactly what he wanted. I caused a scene and made myself look…stupid." She burst into tears again. "My relationship is over. Cade will never forgive me."

Jonathan got up and pulled her into his arms. "Cade loves you, honey. I predict he'll be knocking on that door in a little while. Just give him time to calm down."

Jasmine clung to Jonathan, her tears wetting his sports coat. Arabella's heart ached for the girl. Jasmine had so much love to give. Why did she have to suffer this way?

"Where is Cade now?" she asked Jasmine.

"I don't know. I left him standing in front of the café. But he probably had to go to work."

Jasmine backed away from Jonathan. "I have to go to work, too."

"Why don't you call Deanna and tell her what happened?" Arabella suggested. "Explain that you need some time alone. I'm sure she'll understand."

"No, I'll be okay," Jasmine said. "I don't want to miss work." She sniffed, grabbed a pumpkin-embossed napkin and blew her nose then started for the stairs. "I'm gonna freshen up and get myself together. I don't know what else to do."

Jonathan watched her go. "I can't believe this, but I have to agree with Jasmine. Her ruined dress is a sensitive issue and of course she'd suspect Cade's family. Do you think the wedding is really off?"

"No, I think they'll get through this." Arabella put away the cookies then pulled the biggest of the three cake tiers out of the oven. Next came the center and then the smaller top layer. She placed each on the counter to let them cool. "Those two are crazy in love. Cade will come around. Poor kid. He probably does get tired of hearing people bad-mouth his father and his sneaky uncles. But… Charley gives everyone good ammunition. He's lazy and always complaining. He likes to blame everyone else for his problems. He's a sorry excuse for a father but I guess Cade loves him anyway."

Jonathan thought about his own childhood and his long-dead father. "I loved my father, too. Even after the way he treated us. I wanted so badly to please him, to make him change. But I finally realized I couldn't force the man to do something he wasn't able to do."

Arabella didn't want to press but she had to ask. "Did he…abuse you?"

"Not me," Jonathan said, his eyes downcast. "He took out his rage on Aaron. Aaron tried to protect me and he did most of the time. Then he grew up and got a job. When he wasn't working he was in a bar somewhere, just to stay out of the house, I think." He looked out the window. "So I was on my own. But I couldn't take it anymore after I got older. I left as soon as I could. I don't think Aaron ever got over the way I abandoned him. He was a good brother. I can't say the same for myself."

Arabella thought about what he'd said and how standing at his brother's grave in that same place where they'd both suffered must have affected him this morning, too. "But, Jonathan, it sounds as if he abandoned you first. He turned to drinking to escape. And he never came back for you."

He lifted his head, his eyes bright with misery and acceptance. "I've never thought about it that way. Maybe he wasn't so much angry at me as he was with himself. I wish I'd tried harder to make amends with him, though. I didn't get that chance and now it's too late. He's gone."

"I'm so sorry for you and Jasmine. It's a shame it took so long for you to find each other."

He looked into her eyes, his gratitude shining in his bittersweet smile. "At least I found her safe and happy. I wish she hadn't been abandoned, though."

"I sure know that feeling," Arabella admitted, wishing she knew how to comfort him. "I've often wondered if I'd be closer to my mother now if I'd left with her all those years ago. But then I might not have my girls if I'd done that." She glanced at the clock. "Speaking of that, I need to pick them up from preschool."

Jonathan lifted his head. "Want me to do that?"

"They're not expecting you."

"Then I'll ride with you," he offered.

She thought about it. He didn't seem to have anything urgent to do and Jasmine was going to work anyway, so no need to leave him here with her. The man was as antsy as a caged cat. And no wonder. His niece was in crisis and he'd just stood over his brother's grave. In her usual pragmatic way, Arabella decided to keep him busy. "Okay. Let me check on Jasmine and get my purse."

She found Jasmine sitting on the window seat in her room. The newborn sunlight shot through the sheers to send a glow over the strewn clothes lying across the floral, ruffled bedspread. The walls were covered with pictures of Jasmine and Cade, smiling and happy, at football games and the prom and, later, graduation. Jasmine would never get over it if Cade broke her heart. "Are you okay, honey?"

Jasmine nodded then changed that to shaking her head. "I love Cade so much. What am I gonna do now? My daddy died without me ever really knowing him and now I might not have a life with Cade."

Arabella sat down beside her and took her hand. "Cade is just angry and hurt right now. In his heart, he knows you have a right to accuse his family. They certainly haven't welcomed you with open arms. Have you tried calling him?"

"No. He made it clear he didn't want to talk to me." She wiped at her eyes again. "And to make it even worse, Pauley was standing there watching with this smirk on his face. He actually clapped when he heard Cade telling me to get out of his face."

Arabella wanted to find Pauley Clayton and throttle the man. Why couldn't her family be normal? Why did they all have to be so dysfunctional and melodramatic? "Pauley is full of bluster, honey. If he'd do a better job as mayor, this town might actually get back on track."

"That doesn't make me feel any better," Jasmine said, getting up to find a tissue. "I've got to go. I'm already late but I'm pretty sure Deanna will know the reason why. I saw Katrina going into the shop with your cousin Marsha right after my fight with Cade. And honestly, your mother had the same smirk on her face as Pauley had."

Arabella thought about Jasmine's revelation while she and Jonathan loaded up the girls. She should have asked Jasmine to clarify why she distrusted Katrina so much, but Jasmine had shut down after making that telling remark. But Jasmine was right about the whole town buzzing with the news of the disagreement between Jasmine and Cade. Arabella had already had calls from Brooke and Kylie. The word was out all over town that Cade and Jasmine had broken up. Arabella had been against this wedding before, but now she was determined to make it happen. Didn't Jasmine deserve something good and precious in her life?

Jonathan touched a finger to Jamie's nose. "All fastened in."

Jamie gave him a smile. "All done."

Arabella had noticed the growing bond between her quietest child and Jonathan. Jamie seemed to run to Jonathan more and more as she got to know him. They'd all miss him when he was gone. She didn't want to think about that today.

"Want to stop for ice cream?" he asked after getting into the front seat with her.

Arabella glanced in the rearview mirror. "No, not today. I can't take having to answer all the questions I'm sure to get. And I have to get that cake decorated so I can deliver it to the church fellowship hall first thing tomorrow."

He glanced back at the girls and winked. "I think we need to grill some cheese sandwiches for lunch."

"I want one," Jessie said, kicking her feet in the air.

"Me, too, Dr. Jon-Thon," Julie replied. She still wasn't as friendly with Jonathan as her sisters, but she was coming around.

"How about you, Jamie?" He reached back to grab her purple boot.

"Cheese, cheese," Jamie chanted. "Can I have some milk with mine, Mommy?"

"Yes, you *may*," Arabella replied. "And maybe a carrot stick or two."

There was more talk about lunch, making her realize Jonathan was right. Her whole family talked about food all the time. She needed to get out more. Preferably doing something that didn't involve food. She thought of dancing in Jonathan's arms and decided maybe she'd do best to stick to cooking and eating.

"Hey, it'll be all right," he said, his hand touching her arm.

Had he read her mind? "I know. I've had to field questions all day, though. First about Lucas. My cousins are worried about him. And now this. We have to put the wedding plans on hold until we see if Cade and Jasmine work things out."

"Okay, let's get home and...when nap time comes, you and I will ice the cake."

The man was a constant surprise. "You don't know how to do that."

"I'm good with a knife—a surgical knife. I think I can get frosting on a cake."

"We'll see. Thanks for the offer."

They pulled into the driveway and unloaded the girls, everyone dragging backpacks and new drawings to go with the rest pasted all over the house.

Arabella made it through the front door, her attention on her children. Jonathan followed up the rear.

Jessie stopped a foot inside the kitchen. "Mommy, what happened to your cake?"

Arabella put away coats and lined up the backpacks. "I took it out of the oven to ice, honey. It's fine."

"No, it's not," Jessie insisted. "It's all crumpled."

"What—?"

Jonathan held Arabella by the arm then pointed to the counter. "She's right. Your cake had been smashed. And...the back door is open."

"What am I going to tell the Burfords?" Arabella asked after she'd cleaned up the big clumps of yellow cake that had been strewn all over the kitchen.

Jonathan finished taking sandwich remains to the sink. He had the girls tucked into their beds for their afternoon naps, but the excitement of finding cake all over the kitchen had them hyped up and scared. The nursery monitor was nearby in case they couldn't settle down. Now he just needed to get their mother settled. She'd gone around cleaning the whole time the girls were eating. At least she'd called Zach. He'd come over and examined the back door.

"Same as last night. No forced entry. Somebody has a key to your house, Arabella. Pretty bold to come in here during the day." Zach's next words were grim. "Somebody must be watching the comings and goings around here."

Jonathan agreed with that assessment. And he hated to even think it might be Kat or an angry Cade who'd done this. He'd offered, no, demanded that she allow him to pay for a security system. But after reluctantly checking, Arabella told him it would be weeks before she could get someone to the house.

Jasmine didn't even know about this latest yet. This would set her back, too.

He took the garbage bag full of cake. "Is it too late to bake another set of layers?"

Arabella let out a long breath. "No, but...I don't think I've got it in me." She shrugged then looked out the window. "I've never let down a paying client and they're really counting on that cake."

"When is the dinner?"

"Tomorrow night."

"That gives us twenty-four hours."

"It's not your job, Jonathan."

"I'm going to help you and you might as well get used to the idea. If I have to find the recipe and bake the cake myself, I'll do it."

She actually smiled at that. "I'm trying to imagine you baking a cake."

"Then help me. We can do this, Arabella. Don't let them win, whoever it is."

"You're sure stubborn. First security and now this."

"So I've been told."

"Okay," she finally said. "Thank goodness I did my bread orders before I baked the cake. If you don't mind staying here with the girls, I'll get my deliveries done this afternoon instead of waiting until tomorrow. That'll leave the rest of tonight and the morning to get the anniversary cake ready."

"Good. Anything else on the agenda?"

"No, not until Cade and Jasmine make up. If they ever do. No need to meet with Kylie and Brooke about the rest of the wedding plans until things settle down. I'm pretty sure this will blow over and Cade will come calling again, but who knows?" She held her hands on her hips. "I can't let it end like this, though. I might have to sit those two down and explain what being adults means."

"Okay, then," Jonathan said, glad to get her back into fight mode. "I'll stay with the girls and you take care of your deliveries. See, we've got it all worked out."

Arabella put the trash bag by the door. "Everything except who's messing with this house."

Jonathan put the broom and dustpan away then turned to face her. "We'll keep working on that, too. Zach said he'd look into matters, but I can ask around, see if any of the neighbors saw anything." He came to stand in front of her. "And I'm working on speeding things up with the security company."

"Thank you," Arabella said. And then she reached up and kissed him on the cheek. "I appreciate it."

Before Jonathan could follow through with a longer kiss, she pivoted and started gathering her delivery baskets. He went to help, but the very air seemed to sizzle from that little peck on the cheek. If helping to bake a cake could bring about this kind of reaction, he wondered what else he could do to help make things better for her. Maybe he'd start by having a long talk with Cade. Man to man.

He wanted Jasmine and Cade to be happy again and he wanted Arabella to get some rest and not have to worry so much, so he'd find out who was behind these attacks and try to make them stop. Because now more than ever, he was willing to do whatever it took to make Arabella Michaels his own.

Chapter Seventeen

He decided to call Cade's cell phone, thinking Cade should be at work out on the Circle C Ranch. From what Jonathan had heard, it was a pretty big working ranch owned and operated by Cody Jameson. He'd rather ride out there, but he couldn't leave the sleeping girls. Staring at the baby monitor, he dialed Cade's cell phone. He'd found the number on Arabella's bulletin board next to the refrigerator.

"Hello?" Cade sounded winded and frustrated.

"Cade, it's Jonathan Turner. We need to talk. Do you have a few minutes?"

"Yes." Silence followed by a long sigh. "I messed up big-time, didn't I?"

"I don't know. But I'd like to help. Do you still love Jasmine?"

"Of course. It's just all this family stuff getting in the way. I didn't mean to get so mad this morning but this makes me crazy." He exhaled wearily. "I shouldn't have taken it out on Jasmine, though.

And especially on the day y'all went to visit her dad's grave."

Jonathan smiled into his cell phone. Cade sounded miserable. "I understand. Finding that wedding dress out in the rain made all of us angry. And people tend to jump to conclusions when they're hurt and angry."

"Jasmine was sure hurt. She was crying. I'm mad because, deep down, I think she might be right. What if someone from my family did this?"

Jonathan had to tread lightly. He wouldn't accuse Cade's family without proof. "We don't know that. But I do need to ask you a question and I want you to be honest."

"I'll try."

"Did you ever give or loan the spare key Arabella gave you to anyone?"

"No, sir. She only gave me that key a few months ago so I could help on the renovations for the apartment. She didn't trust the contractor so I was supposed to supervise things when she couldn't be there. I let them in then helped out where they needed me. Then I shut the house back up and left." He paused. "I only had to use the key a few times, but she told me to keep it. Said I was a good handyman and she might hire me again sometime."

And probably find odd jobs for Cade so she could pay him without wounding his pride. "So you never left it where someone might take it and have a copy made?"

"No, not that I can remember. I told Zach all of this already. My key is in my wallet. Why does everybody think I'm involved in this?"

"I don't think that," Jonathan replied. This was getting him nowhere. "But I do think someone has been watching the house and then coming and going when everyone is out. And they'd have to have a way to get inside undetected."

"Why don't you ask Arabella's mother, then?" Cade shot back. "She's been back a few days and all of this happens. That makes more sense to me. Especially when she's as much as told Jasmine we'd never make it to the altar."

After asking Cade to explain that, Jonathan invited Cade to help him fix Darlene's porch later in the week, but he hung up with no more answers than when he'd started. Cade had promised Jasmine he wouldn't tell Arabella how rude her mother had been to Jasmine and him. But he did tell Jonathan that he was coming by to apologize to Jasmine after he got off work.

At least Jonathan could let Arabella know that. He didn't like all the undercurrents and secrets floating around this town. Somebody sure wanted to upset Arabella's household and stop this wedding. And he had a feeling this was just the beginning.

* * *

Arabella had two more deliveries to make. She'd left some bread at the church pantry to help with the shelter needs. Now she needed to drop off a basket of cookies to Deanna's salon for a staff party that afternoon.

She parked across from Hair Today and got out, taking the mixture of chocolate chip, oatmeal and sugar cookies out of the back of her van. Maybe she'd see Jasmine and find out that she and Cade had made up.

Or maybe not.

Marsha Harris's car was parked in front of the salon. Was today her regular day to get her hair washed and teased? Vincent's sister dressed like a rock star and smoked like a barbecue grill. Her blond hair was usually stringy and so dried out that it practically crinkled. Arabella tried to avoid her cousin because Marsha had bullied Arabella during their school years, and Arabella had always fought back. But there was no way to avoid her today.

Arabella decided she could deal with Marsha, but with the mood she was in right now, Marsha might not be able to deal with her. The tension in the air around here didn't bode well for anyone. How could a simple wedding cause so much havoc?

Because it's not just about the wedding, she thought. No, this latest act of vandalism surely had to do with that will and her grandfather's strange stipulations. Money could do that to people. Sometimes Arabella wished she didn't need that money so much. It would be better for all of them if it just went away.

Why put Jasmine and Cade through this when the will had nothing to do with their wedding?

Bracing herself, Arabella entered the salon, the smell of hair spray and coloring solution assaulting her.

"Hey, there," Deanna called, her smile pretty and her makeup heavy. "Oh, what a lovely basket, Arabella. We'll sure enjoy that this afternoon."

"My pleasure," Arabella said, nodding hello to the few customers sitting under dryers or having their nails done. "I'll put it in the break room." She glanced around, looking for Jasmine.

"She rushed into the back," Marsha offered, her kohl-rimmed eyes moving over Arabella with disdain before she returned to the celebrity magazine she held in her hand. "Fine mess, this supposed wedding between her and Cade. I'm glad he came to his senses. And I told her so." She glanced around as if to dare anyone to dispute her.

Deanna shot Arabella a frown. "Jasmine's upset about that dress and her fight with Cade." She glared at Marsha. "Especially because someone had to go and rub it in. I told her to take a break."

"I'll talk to her," Arabella said, sending Marsha her own frown. "Thanks, Deanna."

"No problem. I was sorry to hear about her daddy dying. She's a good kid."

"Yes, she is. And Cade loves her so much. Too bad somebody had to take it upon themselves to mess things up."

"Yeah, too bad," Marsha said, her tone dripping with sarcasm. "I declare, I don't understand why everybody's so up in arms about those two. This was bound to happen. Better now than after they'd made a big mistake."

Arabella ignored her cousin and headed for the back. Sure enough, she found Jasmine sitting there staring at her cell phone, her eyes red and swollen.

"Honey, why don't you come home with me?"

Jasmine sniffed and looked up. "I'm okay. Cade called me. He's coming to see me after work. He's not mad anymore."

"Well, that's a good thing, right?"

Jasmine nodded. "Yes. But what if his family keeps coming between us? What if it gets worse after we get married? They don't like me at all."

Arabella sat down on a chair across from Jasmine. "Cade loves you. That's really all that matters. But I understand why you're so worried. You know, maybe moving away would be the best thing for both of you. You'd certainly have a better chance at a good education away from here." She swallowed hard, knowing how difficult it was going to be to let her go. "Jonathan is willing to help both of you find jobs and get settled in a good college. I know you wanted to stay here awhile so you could save money, but it might be better if you go wherever Cade goes instead of waiting."

Jasmine looked down at the twisted tissue in her hands. "I never thought I'd want to move away permanently, but I think you're right. I can't stay here, even after we're married. If Cade goes away to school, I can't deal with his family. I didn't want to be separated from him anyway. I guess we'll figure out the financial stuff once we get out there on our own."

Arabella took Jasmine's hands in hers. "I think that's the smart thing to do, and knowing Jonathan is willing to guide you makes me feel better about that. I'll miss you so much…but I want you to be happy."

Jasmine bobbed her head. "I'll miss you, too. But…Uncle Jonathan likes you a lot. You can come and visit us in Denver. Maybe even…strike up a relationship with him, huh?" She nudged Arabella with a gentle fist to her elbow. "You know, a *romantic* relationship."

Hope radiated from Jasmine's puffy eyes. Hope Arabella didn't want to encourage. "Oh, now don't go getting excited about that. I live here. He lives in Denver. It's hard to have any kind of romantic relationship with three little girls, let alone trying to have a long-distance relationship on top of things. It would never work."

Jasmine shrugged then dabbed at her eyes with a fresh tissue. She stood and looked down at Arabella. "People think Cade and I will never work, but we will. You can't give up, Arabella. Uncle Jonathan's got a thing for you. Everyone can see that."

"Really now?" Arabella stood to leave, the thought of Jonathan thinking about her in those terms making her quiver. "I think you're hoping for something that can't be, honey."

"But I won't give up hope," Jasmine replied, her attitude back. "I almost did this morning. It was hard, seeing my dress ruined. Even harder to go to my daddy's grave. Then the fight with Cade and… then Marsha coming in here all smug and talking about how glad she was that Cade had seen the light."

"The nerve of that woman!"

"Yeah…she really crosses the line. And how the gossip got started so fast is beyond me because Cade and I never said the wedding was off—at least not to each other. But people sure did jump to that conclusion." Her lips twisted into a half smile. "But I prayed and prayed for God to show me the way. Then Cade called me and apologized. I love him even more now." Her eyes watered up again.

"And I don't care about the dress. I just want to marry Cade."

Arabella took Jasmine in her arms and hugged her tight. "We'll find you another dress, but I agree that doesn't matter so much now. You know what's important. And that's the first step to a solid marriage. That and keeping the Lord as the center of your unity."

She didn't like reminding herself that she and Harry sure hadn't done that. She'd tried, but Harry had scoffed at any attempts at a true faith. Come to think of it, Harry had pretty much scoffed at any attempts to make the marriage work.

"Thanks," Jasmine said, smiling for the first time that day. "You always make me feel better about things."

Arabella hugged her again. "Now get back to work. And just ignore Marsha. She's bitter because she's not so happy in her marriage. That sorry Billy Dean can barely hold down a job."

"I'll keep that in mind," Jasmine retorted. "I feel better now." She squared her shoulders and headed back out onto the salon floor.

Arabella walked back into the beauty salon, following Jasmine. "Your basket is on the table, Deanna."

"Thanks again," Deanna said. "Do I owe you any more money?"

"No, the check you gave me covered everything."

"Great. See you later, Arabella."

Arabella had her hand on the door when Marsha called to her. "Hey, tell Katrina I sure enjoyed seeing her at lunch the other day."

Shocked, Arabella tried to maintain her cool. "I sure will. It's good she has…friends to visit with while she's here."

"We're more than friends," Marsha said, her tone a bit more shrill this time. "We're family."

"Of course you are," Arabella replied. She waved a goodbye to the room in general then got out before Marsha could form a comeback.

Once she was in her car, Arabella let out the breath she'd been holding. Her mother had always been flighty and reckless, but meeting with Marsha took the cake. Katrina hated Marsha Harris. Was her mother trying to make amends with her family? Or was she keeping her enemies close for a reason?

Arabella couldn't believe her eyes.

She stood at the door, taking in the neatness of her home. The floors gleamed. The furniture was polished. The kitchen was spotless.

And a handsome doctor was on the floor, giving instructions on how to examine a patient to her three girls. In fact, he seemed to *be* the patient.

"Now, Julie, take the stethoscope and hold it right here." Jonathan pointed to his chest. "Listen. Can you hear my heart beating?"

Julie giggled. "I can. I can. It's really loud!"

"I want to try," Jessie said, muscling in on her sister, the ruffle on her long-sleeved yellow sweater hanging over Jonathan's nose.

"Next," Jonathan replied, nodding to Julie to pass the heavy stethoscope to her sister. "Jessie, can you do the same thing Julie did?"

"Yes, sir," Jessie said, using her manners for once. Her brow furrowing underneath the riot of curls surrounding her heart-shaped face, she widened her eyes and listened intently. "You sound like a horse running."

"Yes, it does kind of sound that way." Jonathan glanced at Jamie. "Do you want a turn?"

Jamie shook her head. But she did lift the stethoscope off her sister's tiny shoulders.

"Come on. Try it," Jonathan coaxed, reaching out to tickle Jamie's nose. "You can take my temperature, too."

"Okay." Jamie went to work, her expression so serious Arabella had to smile. After she'd listened to Jonathan's heartbeat, Jamie grabbed the thermometer from his bag and shoved it into his mouth. "You have to wait!" she told him in a stern little voice.

"Oh-kay," Jonathan said through the thermometer, making all the girls peal with laughter.

Arabella advanced into the room. "Oh, my. Do we have a sick person in this house?"

"Mommy!" Jessie hurled herself against Arabella's leg. "Dr. Jon-thon has a tummyache."

"Does he now?" Arabella grinned down at Jonathan. "Have you been in the cookie jar again, Doctor?"

"Yes, ma'am," he said, making a face. "I think I ate too many chocolate-chip cookies and bread pudding."

The girls looked from Jonathan to their mother, obviously interested in her reaction to that admission.

"I see. Well, then I guess I'll have to hide those cookies again and keep you out of the pudding. And give you some tummy medicine, too."

Jamie leaned over Jonathan. "Now you're in trouble, mister."

Jonathan rolled over and lifted Jamie in the air. "I guess I am." He had the child giggling and begging to be put down. He gently lowered her, making a sound like a crane. "There you go. Back on solid ground."

Arabella didn't think her heart was quite back down to earth, however. The sight of her girls playing with Jonathan caused her to soar into the clouds. But she needed to settle down and remember what she'd told Jasmine earlier. A city man would never settle for the small-town girl—plus three.

"Whew, I'm exhausted." Jonathan hopped up to face Arabella. "How are you?"

"I'm okay." She kissed each of the girls and scooted them toward their toys.

Jonathan gathered everything back into his bag. "They had a good nap and then we had cookies and milk. I could get used to this." He looked over at Arabella as if he'd realized he'd said that out loud. "I mean that. I think I could really get used to this."

Arabella couldn't breathe, so she retreated to her kitchen. Her clean, sparkling kitchen. "So could I," she mumbled to herself.

When she turned around, Jonathan was right behind her. The yearning look in his eyes told her he'd heard her. The soft smile on his face told her he agreed.

Chapter Eighteen

Jonathan stared at the array of mixing bowls and baking pans Arabella had spread out across the counter. "So you know what to do with all of this, right?"

"Don't look so panicked," she said with an impish glance. "I've been doing this for a long time."

He swallowed, wondering exactly when he'd started falling for her. "I know, I know. It's just like operating. Or at least I've tried to tell myself that. Except we have to put all of this together to create something. Whereas I usually have to fix something and keep my patient intact."

"Same principles." She sifted cake flour and measured accordingly. "We both have to be good at our jobs."

"I only hope we can be good at this together."

There it was again. That tense, heightened silence.

He had to stop making these remarks that implied other things. They were baking a big cake. Nothing more.

But something sure was cooking between them.

He tried again. "So...the girls are down for the count, and Jasmine and Cade have made up and are out for an evening stroll. All is well with our world for now, right?"

"You forgot my mother," she retorted, her frustrations on that subject obvious. "She's avoiding me, thankfully."

Jonathan watched as she cranked up the big mixer. When she gave him the nod, he dropped in the ingredients one at a time. "She was quiet at dinner."

Arabella pursed her lips, watching the mixture turn from flour mixed with butter, sugar and eggs to a creamy yellow concoction that would make a layer. "I tried to corner her to ask her what she'd said to Jasmine and why she's hanging out with Marsha, but she played coy with me. If I didn't have to redo this cake, I'd be up in her room right now getting some answers."

Jonathan waited until she turned off the mixer. "She seemed shocked when you told her you were changing all the locks."

"That's because she probably gave someone a spare key to get in here."

"Do you really think your own mother is behind these vandalism acts?"

She dropped the pumpkin-embossed dish towel. "I don't want to believe that, but things have started going wrong ever since she came home." She shrugged. "Of course, Kitty Kat implied you'd had every opportunity to ruin the wedding, too."

"That's ridiculous. First, she agrees the bride and groom should move to Denver with me, and now she's accusing me?"

"My mother is a piece of work." Arabella poured the first batch of batter into the biggest of the tiered pans. "After I get this cake done, I'm going to talk to her. If not tonight, then first thing tomorrow morning." She wiped at the counter and started measuring for the second layer. "You know, she agrees with you on one subject at least. She hinted that Macy Perry might be a Clayton."

Jonathan started washing measuring cups and wooden spoons. "I can't prove it, but it all adds up. She looks like a Clayton and…Darlene is very tight-lipped whenever I mention any of you Claytons. The timing makes sense, too."

"Yes, I agree. That timing also coincides with when my mother left town. She said my grandfather paid her off. I wonder if this is the secret she's keeping. But that doesn't explain why she's become so chummy with Marsha and our other cousins."

"Maybe she had a pact with Darlene. Darlene told me she promised to never reveal the father."

"I don't know. But I'm going to find out somehow." She wiped her hands then turned on the mixer. "Let's change the subject."

Seeing her agitation, Jonathan did just that. He talked about the girls and how he enjoyed playing with them. He told her about the couple of patients he'd seen yesterday at the church. He also told her he and Cade planned to fix Darlene's front porch tomorrow.

"I've discussed this with Reverend West, but I think while I'm here…and maybe after I go back to Denver, too, I'd like to take one afternoon a week and set up a free clinic at the church. For those who come through needing help or anyone who can't pay."

Arabella stopped the mixer so he could pour in the sugar. "Jonathan, that's a great idea. We sure need that in this economy. A lot of people around here are out of work. They can't afford to see a doctor."

She smiled over at him, her gold-flecked brown eyes rivaling any sunset he'd ever seen. Not able to take his eyes off her, he held the sugar while she turned the mixer back on. But he missed the bowl and sugar sprinkled all over the counter.

"Oh, sorry," he said, reaching for the dish towel at the same time she did.

Their hands met, his over hers. Instead of pulling away, Jonathan took her hand and pulled it up to his chest. "You have flour on your face," he said, reaching his other hand up to brush away the white spot.

Arabella's gaze locked with his as he drew close.

It was now or never, Jonathan decided. Without stopping to think about the consequences, he leaned close, his hand still on her cheek, and kissed her. She stiffened at first but then something incredible happened. Arabella held his other hand and wrapped her free arm around his neck to pull him close.

She tasted of cinnamon and sweetness, better than any of the cookies he'd sampled from her kitchen. She felt warm and small in his arms, making him want to hold her and protect her for a very long time.

But…he didn't have much time. And he couldn't ask her to change her whole life for him.

Jonathan pulled away to stare down at her. "I think I'm beginning to enjoy baking."

Arabella tried to straighten her hair. "It's…not smart to distract the cook."

"Am I a distraction?"

She focused on the batter. "You know you are. What if I came to stand in your operating room?"

He thought about that. "I'd be so shaky I wouldn't be able to hold a scalpel."

"Exactly."

"I'm only trying to help."

She grabbed the sugar and slung it into the big

mixing bowl. "I'm too confused to think right now, Jonathan. There's so much going on around here. You came at the worst possible time. But then, I'm not sure there is a good time for so many changes. I'm not good with change."

He leaned close, pulled her hands away from the mixer.

"You mean there's too much going on between us?"

"Yes. We're not thinking straight."

"My mind was very clear just now when I kissed you," he murmured.

To prove that point he did it again, his lips hitting on hers with all the churning of that souped-up mixing machine.

Then he pulled back to whisper, "You're making something sweet with that mixer. And I'm finding something sweet in your kisses. What's to figure out about that?"

She turned away, her hands on the counter. "Kissing is fine and dandy. But regret is hard to swallow."

"So you regret kissing me?"

"Not now. But I will. You'll be gone soon. Gone. And I'll be left alone. My girls will keep me busy and I'm blessed to have them. I love them so much. But I won't have Jasmine and I won't have you. That's gonna be hard. Real hard."

He tugged her back around. "Ah, but Jasmine

cares about you and loves you. She won't forget your kindness to her. And...I know the way back to you, Arabella."

She looked hopeful at first, her eyes shimmering in a golden halo. Then she gave him one of her pragmatic stares. "That's a long road, Jonathan. A very long road."

Then she turned back to her work, her doubts and regrets swirling with every turn of the mixing blades.

Jonathan's cell phone jingled, bringing Arabella out of her mortified stupor. Why couldn't she face the man?

Listening to his deep voice as he talked to the caller, Arabella rethought the amazing kiss they'd just shared. She'd never again look at her mixing bowl in the same way.

Oh, mercy, I'm in such trouble, she thought, her mind churning as she remembered the warmth of his lips on hers and the way he held her as if she were the only woman on earth. That kiss had elevated her feelings for Jonathan way above the safety level. She was now in the clouds, dreaming about things she couldn't have. And that was dangerous.

"I have to leave for a little while."

From somewhere below her perch above the earth, Arabella heard Jonathan's voice in her ear.

She spun around so fast, she splattered cake batter on his shirt.

"Oh, I'm so sorry." Grabbing the dish towel, she dabbed at the creamy blob.

Jonathan took her hand, stilling her. "Arabella, I have to go out to the Circle C to check on some workers who are sick." He watched her, probably to make sure she'd comprehended what he'd just said. "Will you be all right? I don't like leaving you with all these break-ins."

Embarrassed, she tugged her hands away. "Of course. I'm used to being alone, remember? I'm used to baking my cakes and pies late at night, right by my lonesome. You don't have to worry about me. Go on."

"I intend to find out who did this, destroying that dress and ruining your cake. I mean that."

"No, you don't need to do that, Jonathan. I told you, I can take care of myself."

His jaw tightened. "You don't want my help?"

She wanted his help, yearned for more of his kisses, but this was her battle to fight. "I...I can't press charges against my kin. It's that simple."

"You're kidding, right?"

"I don't have a choice. If you interfere, it could make things worse. Please don't get involved."

He stared at her, blinking in confusion. "Arabella, I *am* involved. We need to talk about everything, starting with that kiss, I think. We need to talk about…us."

She slammed drawers open and shut then threw spoons and other utensils into the sink, hoping the noise would drown out her obvious despair. "Nothing to discuss. Go check on your patient."

He didn't look so sure but he walked backward toward the door. "I'll be back as soon as I can."

"Take your time. I'm just gonna piddle around until these layers are done and out of the oven. I might be asleep when you get home—when you get back."

He came close again, his face inches from hers. "We're not done here, Arabella."

"I think we are," she retorted. "Jonathan, we both know this can't work. You belong in Denver. I'm happy here."

"We could try," he said. "Denver's not that far away."

"But your mind-set is. You don't want to be here. You've made that very clear. And I can't…go there."

"You have no idea what my mind-set is or what I want," he said, his tone now full of anger and hurt. "I think you're using every excuse you can find to avoid the truth—about your family and about me. We can work this out if you'll give me a chance."

Arabella couldn't speak. He wanted a chance? She didn't think she could base their future on a chance.

"Arabella?"

She turned back to the mixer. "I have to get this cake done. And you need to go."

He headed toward the back door. A minute later she heard the engine of his fancy car revving up.

"My, my, what you got cooking in this kitchen, girl?"

Arabella whirled around to find her mother standing there, her arms folded over her zebra-print pajamas, a smug look on her face.

"I'm re-baking the tiered layers for the Burfords' cake, Mom. You know, the cake that someone managed to toss all over my kitchen earlier today."

"I'm not talking about any cake," Katrina replied before she slinked onto a stool to stare at Arabella. "Where'd your doctor go?"

Arabella dropped the wooden spoon she'd used to spread batter. "Were you spying on us?"

"No, but I heard the last of it. Somebody's been kissing the cook around here." She made a tsk-tsk sound. "And the cook, as usual, is being way too sensible about things."

"You're impossible," Arabella said, fatigue cloaking her. She was tired of fighting her mother and her cousins. She was tired of fighting her feelings for Jonathan. And she was tired of being tired all the time. "You won't talk to me about why you're here and what's going on, but you question me about kissing Jonathan. What is the matter with you?"

Katrina leaned across the counter. "Honey, I'm trying to help you out. You should go on to Denver with that good-looking doctor. And take Jasmine and Cade with you."

"You've been trying to get me to leave since you arrived here," Arabella said. "And you're deliberately berating Jasmine. If I didn't know better, I'd think you're trying to get rid of both of us. Why is that, Mama?"

"I want you to be happy," Katrina said, her expression sincere, her words soft. "I've done you wrong, honey. I'm trying to make amends."

"By pushing my children and me out of this house? If you want to live here, just say so."

"I don't want this old house. And you can do better, much better. Think of all the advantages you'd have, being married to a big-city doctor." Katrina's expression turned dreamy but then she snapped back to attention. "And as for Jasmine, she needs a reality check. Love don't always pay the bills."

"Well, maybe that's why I'm not rushing into anything with Jonathan. I have to pay my bills and I've learned I can't depend on anyone else to help me."

"He's loaded, sugarpie."

"You are living in a dream world," Arabella replied, wondering if her mother had been snooping around to get information about Jonathan. "It was just a kiss, not a proposal. Jonathan and I...we're too different. I love it here but he doesn't. He hates the way he grew up. I've always loved living in Clayton. That's why I didn't leave when you did."

"I should have made you."

"You shouldn't have left at all," Arabella said, shocked that she'd finally spoken what had been on her mind for years. She halted, took a breath. "I needed you, Mama. I needed a mother, but you left me. And I've never understood why. Just like I don't understand what you're doing here now."

Katrina came around the counter and placed her hands on Arabella's arms. "I didn't have a choice, honey. I couldn't stay here. I couldn't. I thought I'd be happier out there in the big old world. But I wasn't."

"So you're back now, trying to convince me to make the same mistake? I can't just up and move with three little girls, especially with the will stating we all have to be here. And besides, Jonathan hasn't exactly made it clear if he'd even want me in Denver with him. I can't take that kind of risk."

"He sure acts like he's interested, I can assure you. And I'm trying to convince you to find some peace of mind before it's too late. And, yes, that can be risky but worth the effort. That's why I came back, honey." She released a quavering breath. "My daddy and I hadn't spoken in more than ten years. And now he's dead. Look what happened to

Jonathan and his brother, Jasmine and her daddy. I didn't want things to be that way with us. I wanted to get to know my granddaughters. Is that so wrong?"

"Just tell me," Arabella said, wishing with all her heart she could believe her mother. "Did you have anything to do with Jasmine's wedding dress being destroyed or that cake getting messed up?"

"Of course I didn't," Katrina said, shaking her head. "My own daughter doesn't even trust me." She held her head down, fiddling with the pink ribbon on her pajama top.

"I'm sorry, but you haven't exactly given me any reason to trust you," Arabella said. "And you still haven't explained anything to me. Maybe one day we can be honest with each other, Mama."

Katrina nodded then turned toward the hallway. "One day, honey, it will all make sense, I promise."

But Arabella couldn't accept that promise or her mother's reasons for returning to Clayton. The uneasiness she'd felt since the day she'd approached Jonathan in the church parking lot seemed to double. Jonathan's reasons for coming here were clear now. He wanted a relationship with his niece. Arabella couldn't fault him for that. The poor man had gotten more than he'd bargained for.

But Arabella still couldn't figure out why her mother had returned. She didn't believe her mother had suddenly become concerned in her old age. Katrina wasn't one for making amends.

Her mother had let her down too many times. Her grandfather also had let her down, but at least he'd tried to be kind in the end. Her husband had certainly disappointed her. And her family was constantly at war. No wonder she couldn't trust anyone.

And maybe that was why she couldn't accept that she was falling in love with Jonathan. What if he let her down, too?

After her cake layers were in the oven and her house was blessedly quiet, Arabella sank down at the counter and closed her eyes. She had some serious prayers to send up to the Lord.

And a long list of worries for Him to consider.

Chapter Nineteen

"Food poisoning again?"

Cody Jameson hit his battered cowboy hat against his jeans, his face twisted into a frustrated frown. Running a hand down his five-o'clock shadow, he said, "We've been through this already. I guess I'm gonna have to let that ornery cook go."

Jonathan felt for the rancher. "From what your men told me, that won't be soon enough. Arabella could probably help out until you hire someone permanently." After stating that, Jonathan hurriedly added, "Of course, I can't speak for her."

"I might ask her," Cody said, his hazel eyes gleaming. "I got people to feed. I like to keep my workers happy."

His uncle and right-hand man, Ted Jameson, nodded. "Happens a lot lately. We'll lose all of our employees if we can't provide them with safe, decent meals."

Jonathan had already given the sick men instructions on what to do, and he'd called in some medicine to help see them through the worst. But that wouldn't be ready until in the morning and it would take a long drive to get to the nearest drugstore. "I'm sorry I can't do more."

"You helped a lot," Cody said, extending his hand. "Cade goes on and on about what a great doctor you are. When that boy's not breaking his back working around here, he has his nose in some medical book or journal. He's serious about wanting to be a doctor. And I believe he's got the mind to back it up." He cleared his throat. "At least he had the good sense not to eat his meals here. He's the one who suggested I call you."

"So I hear," Jonathan said with a grin. "I'm doing my best to help him get on the fast track with his education."

"I hope the kid makes it," Cody replied. "Me, I love what I do here but it's hard work." He slid his hat over his sandy-brown curls and glanced over at his uncle. "We really need a cook who can keep the food safe."

Jonathan snapped his fingers. "Hey, Arabella's cousin Vivienne is a chef. She's coming home any day now, according to Arabella. She might be able to help out since she lost her job in New York."

Cody shot his uncle another deep frown then grunted. Tugging his hat back down over his forehead, he said, "I'm not sure Vivienne Clayton would want to work for the Circle C. And to tell the truth, I'd rather not deal with somebody from New York. Period. End of discussion."

Jonathan sensed a shred of disapproval in the words, coupled with the tension that suddenly filled the room. "Well, I hope things work out for you."

He'd be gone soon anyway, he reminded himself as he got in his car. As Arabella had pointed out in her rejection of him, he needed to quit worrying about everyone in Clayton and get back to his own life.

Jonathan left the ranch and drove toward town, his mind spinning with all the possibilities of a life with Arabella. Before he knew it, he'd turned onto Morning Dove Road. When he pulled up to the two-story white house with the for-sale sign, he turned off the car and got out to stare up at the old house.

"Lord, I'm literally at a crossroads here," he said into the moonlit night, hoping his prayers would bring him the answers he needed.

Arabella had turned him down back at the house after that kiss. She didn't need him in her life. But he couldn't let her get away that easily. So he went over his options.

He could go back to Denver and get back to his old routine, all the while preparing for Jasmine and Cade to come there after they were married. That was a good plan and would bring him closer to his niece. And maybe Arabella.

He could resign from the hospital and stay here in Clayton and try his hand at being a country doctor. It wouldn't hurt to brush up on his general studies for that. He wouldn't make much money, but then it didn't seem to take as much money to live here. And he had a good investment plan in place to cover hard times.

Or…he could go back to Arabella and tell her he was falling for her and that he wanted to try and make it work. That would mean going back to Denver now, with the intent of courting her both long-distance and close-up. He could make trips to Clayton on the weekends and his days off. And if she'd just bend a little, she and the girls could come to Denver and visit. It wasn't hard to drive up the interstate. That way she'd still be able to see Jasmine and continue to be a part of her life, too.

But what if she didn't go for that plan? Would he be willing to change his life completely to win her over?

Jonathan glanced around the quiet street, thinking his time here had been so different from the pace of a big-city hospital. A slower pace but still full of chaos at times. Chaos and the joy of walking into a house full of love. Sure, he'd miss the adrenaline rush of emergency surgery. But he'd also found the joy of being needed, the expressions from the hearts of patients who had much more than just money to give him. Could he exchange one form of work for another to receive the nurturing and love he'd never had as a child? To have the family he'd always dreamed about?

It would be hard to give up surgery, but he could keep his privileges at the hospital and maybe contribute now and then. If he knew he'd have Arabella and those precious girls to come home to every night, he could give up just about anything.

The hard part would be convincing Arabella that this was real, that he wasn't playing around. He was in this for the long haul. For the first time in his life he wanted the family he'd tried so hard to push away.

He wanted Arabella and her family.

"Help me, Lord."

Jonathan got back in his car and headed for one more stop before he went back to talk to Arabella.

Maybe Darlene Perry would have some words of wisdom for him.

Surprised to see Reverend West's car parked at Darlene's house, Jonathan hopped out and hurried up onto the porch then knocked at the screen door. He hoped Darlene hadn't taken a turn for the worst.

The reverend greeted him at the door. "Jonathan, we were just talking about you."

"You were?" Jonathan wondered if God had brought him here for a reason. "I hope it was good."

"It was," Reverend West said, slapping him on the back as he ushered Jonathan into the living room. "Darlene has had a good day today. She was bragging on you and credits you with some of that."

Jonathan smiled at Darlene. "Hello. So you're feeling better?"

"A bit," Darlene said, taking his hand in both of hers. "I'm so glad you're here. I wanted to thank you for coming tomorrow to fix the porch. Macy was so tickled about that when I told her yesterday."

Macy came in from the kitchen then, carrying a tray with water and pills on it. "Hi, Dr. Jonathan."

It struck him again how much she reminded him of Arabella's cousin Brooke. "Hey, Macy. How're you doing tonight?"

"Great. Reverend West brought us some videos. Mama and me are gonna watch *The Sound of Music.*"

"With popcorn and lemon-lime soda," Darlene replied with glee. "I have to indulge sometimes, don't I?"

"A little indulgence is good for the soul," Reverend West said, smiling. "I'd better get on home before my wife sends out a patrol. I'll leave you in the doc's hands."

He stood but turned to Jonathan. "Doc, it's sure good to have you here. Have you considered what we talked about?"

Jonathan didn't know what to say. "Yes, sir.

But…I have a lot to work out before I can make that kind of commitment."

"You'll make it work, son. God and I will be right there with you all the way."

Jonathan could believe in that at least. He nodded but remained silent.

"What was that all about?" Darlene asked, her smile as mysterious as the *Mona Lisa*'s.

"The preacher thinks I need to stay here and open a clinic."

"Well, so do I. You've helped me so much. Not with medicine but just by listening to me and…not judging me."

Touched, Jonathan glanced toward Macy. The girl was absorbed in the information on the DVD they planned to watch. "You've had a hard time of it, Darlene. Why would I judge you?"

"You know why," she said, her voice low. "But I made a promise…not so much to the man I loved here on earth. More so to the man above. I promised the Lord I'd do my best by this child and that I'd never make any trouble for anyone else. I've tried my best to abide by that." She settled back on the couch. "But lately I'm beginning to wonder if I made the right decision."

Jonathan had always been on the fringes of faith, hanging back without making a strong commitment. What if he made the wrong decision? Or what if he turned to God for guidance and finally made the right decision, the only decision for his life?

After checking on Darlene's vitals and talking to Macy for a while, Jonathan left the little farmhouse with a new hope in his heart. He drove by the house on Morning Dove Road one more time then decided what he wanted to do. Now he had to convince Arabella it was the right thing for both of them.

She couldn't decide if she wanted the icing to be light blue or creamy white.

Arabella stared at the three perfect layers, wondering how anybody could be devious enough to destroy both a wedding dress and an anniversary cake all in the same week. Whoever had done this would have their own day of reckoning. Right now, she had a cake to decorate.

She decided she'd go with the light blue icing and trim it in the creamy white. Sometimes life was all about compromise.

That thought stopped her in her tracks. She'd shoved Jonathan away because she wasn't willing to compromise. Or because she thought he wasn't willing to commit. Had she lost the best thing that had ever walked through those doors?

Her mother wanted her to take up with Jonathan. Jasmine had hinted at that very thing.

Her cousins pestered her on a daily basis about it.

And even Dorothy Henry had pegged him as a winner right from the start.

So why was Arabella holding back?

"I don't like change," she said on an edge of frustration. And trying to maintain a relationship with Jonathan would mean a big change. That was her best excuse, but it was a sad excuse.

The more she thought about taking things to the next level with Jonathan, the more it made sense. She didn't have to change that much. She could continue to encourage Cade and Jasmine to take Jonathan up on his offer, but that didn't mean she would never see any of them again. Denver wasn't across the world, for goodness sake. It was an hour or so up the road. And maybe it was time for her to step outside of her comfort zone and try driving past the city-limit sign.

"Is this right, Lord?" she prayed. "Should I meet Jonathan halfway and tell him...I'm in love with him?"

When she heard the sound of that purring engine revving in her driveway, Arabella almost dropped a spoonful of blue icing.

Willing her heart to stop jitterbugging, she went back to work on the bottom layer of the cake.

The back door opened and she heard him walking toward her. "Hi," he said as he came around the counter, his wary eyes on her.

"Hey. Everybody okay at the ranch?"

"They will be. Food poisoning. They need a cook. I mentioned your cousin Vivienne."

She had to laugh at that. "Right. Viv is an uptown kind of girl. I can't picture her slinging hash for a bunch of cowhands."

"It was just a thought."

She shouldn't have blurted that out. He was trying to help. He was always trying to help. "Well, you never know."

"No, you never know." He came around the counter and took the wooden spoon out of her hand. "Arabella, we need to talk."

"I'm glad you said that. I agree."

"You do?" he said, surprised.

She did, but her heart might not make it through this conversation. "I've been thinking—"

"Me, too." He tugged her close, his eyes moving over her face. "We can make this work. You don't have to move to Denver. But you can come and visit anytime."

Disappointment filled her soul. He wanted her to come and visit? "Of course I can. Especially if Cade and Jasmine are there."

He leaned close. "Especially if I buy that house that's for sale on Morning Dove Road, the one I told you about. And especially if I open a clinic there and continue to have medical services available once a week at the church, too."

"But that means *you* won't be in Denver."

"Yes, that's what it means. But…I'd keep my apartment in Denver…and I'd keep my privileges at the hospital so I could do surgery there. My patients here could go there for more extensive procedures." He smiled down at her. "And…that means that after we're married, we can go to the city anytime and visit Jasmine and Cade. You don't have to lose anyone, Arabella. And you don't have to be alone anymore."

Her heart was tripping over that "after we're married" part. "No, I don't, do I?" She swallowed, blinking back tears. "I'd decided I could drive up the interstate more often if it meant being closer to you. I want to be closer to you, Jonathan. Somehow."

His smile radiated with hope and relief. "I think we're on the same page here."

"Yes, I'd say we are."

"So, we get the kids married and settled and then…we plan our future? I won't pursue going after your relatives. I'll leave that up to the authorities. That way I can concentrate on…*our* family."

She loved the sound of those words. "I think that might work."

He reached out to brush away a sprig of hair on her temple. "I won't force you into anything you can't handle. It's a change but it'll be a gradual change."

That he was willing to take things slowly made her want to hurry toward their life together.

Arabella reached into the icing bowl and touched

a blue glob to his nose. "Not fast enough for me, Dr. Jon-Thon."

He laughed, rubbed his nose against hers then kissed her, smearing blue icing all over both of them. Then he lifted his head and grinned down at her. "I love you. I've never said that to a woman before."

"I love you, too." Arabella smiled back at him then gently wiped the icing off his jawline. "And I've never heard those words sound so good."

He hugged her tight. "Are we crazy?"

"Having doubts already?"

"No. I just can't believe how lucky I am."

"Lucky to fall for a woman who lives in a creaky old Victorian house and has triplet girls and really strange relatives? Yeah, right."

He kissed her again then held her head in his hands. "Speaking of those girls, can we go and check on them? I've never actually seen them asleep."

"They're at their best when they lay there like little angels."

"Our angels," he said, taking her hand to lead her upstairs. "A beautiful family."

Arabella turned on the stairs. "If you survived the past couple of weeks, I guess you can survive anything."

He pulled her head down. "I didn't just survive. I thrived, Arabella." He kissed her. "And I'm happy."

She was happy, too.

The front door opened and Jasmine and Cade came in carrying a big box. "This was on the porch. A delivery." Jasmine stopped to stare at them. "What's going on?"

Jonathan grabbed the box. "Oh, good. It's here."

"What's going on?" Jasmine asked again, her gaze moving from Arabella to Jonathan.

"We're in love," Jonathan replied. "Now open this, Jasmine."

Giving him a questioning look, Jasmine tore into the big box and pulled back the tissue paper. "Oh, oh," she said as she tugged at the delicate satin. "It's a wedding dress. Arabella, it looks almost exactly like the one you made for me."

Arabella couldn't stop the tears. "It sure does. Jonathan ordered it for you, honey."

Cade looked at Jonathan then back to Jasmine, shielding his eyes with his hand. "Don't let me see it. It's bad luck."

They all laughed at that. Jasmine closed the box then rushed into Jonathan's arms. "Thank you so much." Then she stood back. "Wait? Did you say y'all are in love?"

Jonathan nodded. "We'll explain later."

He took Arabella's hand and they went upstairs to the big room next to the master bedroom and stood in the door watching Jessie, Jamie and Julie sleep.

"Beautiful," Jonathan said, holding Arabella close.

"Your new family," Arabella replied. "Are you sure about this?"

"Oh, yeah."

The dread she'd felt for so long vanished in a cloud of pure joy. She sent up prayers of hope for the rest of her family, especially Lucas. But for now, she couldn't stop the bliss spilling over inside her heart.

Maybe change wasn't such a bad thing after all.

* * * * *

Dear Reader,

It was a joy to be a part of this big, sprawling story of the Clayton family. I've been to Colorado a few times and I love the state, but trying to keep up with the Claytons was a new experience! Thanks to all the other writers on this project for keeping me on track!

My heroine, Arabella Michaels, is independent and determined. She wants to protect her three little girls, but in doing so, she guards her heart a bit too closely.

Dr. Jonathan Turner secretly wants a family of his own, but he also guards his true feelings by pouring himself into work. When he comes to Clayton looking for his niece, not only does he find family but he also finds a ready-made family in Arabella and her adorable four-year-old triplets. The city doctor falls for the small-town girl…and her children.

I believe there are families all over the world who have merged to become a true family. I know this isn't always easy. But to those who work hard on being a family, I salute you. God had only one son and that son came to teach us how to love and how to find redemption. We are never alone when we have Christ by our side. I hope you enjoyed this colorful story. Keep in touch with me at www.lenoraworth.com.

Until next time, may the angels watch over you, always.

Lenora Worth

Questions for Discussion

1. Why did Jonathan Turner show up in Clayton? Do you think he did the right thing by coming to see his niece? Why or why not?

2. Arabella couldn't trust him at first. How did she handle this and why do you think she didn't trust him?

3. Arabella had a lot of responsibilities—her triplet girls, a bakery business and a "foster" daughter who was determined to get married. Do you think Arabella handled this in a good way? Have you ever had this kind of responsibility? How did you deal with it?

4. Arabella married young and regretted it (even though she didn't regret having her triplets). What advice would you give to a young bride?

5. Do you think Jasmine and Cade were too young to get married? Do you know someone who married young and remained together? How did they make it work?

6. Arabella's grandfather seemed to be a mean old man, but she knew another side of George

Clayton. Do you think Grandpa had a soft spot for Arabella? If so, how did he show it?

7. Arabella's family had a long history of feuding and fighting. Have you experienced such things with your family? How did you handle this?

8. Arabella wasn't close to her mother, but Katrina returned and settled into Arabella's household anyway. How would you feel if a relative you didn't get along with showed up at your door?

9. Why do you think Katrina came back to Clayton? Did you find any redeeming qualities in her? If so, what were they?

10. Jonathan's attitude toward small-town life slowly began to change after he'd been in Clayton for a while. Have you ever experienced this when moving to a new place? Explain.

11. Jonathan was a surgeon in Denver. Do you think he could make it in a small-town general practice? Do you know a doctor who enjoys this type of work?

12. Together, Arabella and Jonathan worked to create a future for Jasmine and Cade. They compromised in order to do what was right for

those they loved. Have you ever had to deal with a situation such as this? What happened?

13. Would you ever move to a town like Clayton? Why or why not?

14. Do you have family members you've grown apart from? How could you go about reconnecting? Would you even want to?

15. Who do you think is orchestrating all the pranks in Clayton? And why?

LARGER-PRINT BOOKS!

GET 2 FREE
LARGER-PRINT NOVELS
PLUS 2 FREE
MYSTERY GIFTS

Love Inspired

Larger-print novels are now available...

YES! Please send me 2 FREE LARGER-PRINT Love Inspired® novels and my 2 FREE mystery gifts (gifts are worth about $10). After receiving them, if I don't wish to receive any more books, I can return the shipping statement marked "cancel". If I don't cancel, I will receive 6 brand-new novels every month and be billed just $4.99 per book in the U.S. or $5.49 per book in Canada. That's a saving of at least 23% off the cover price. It's quite a bargain! Shipping and handling is just 50¢ per book in the U.S. and 75¢ per book in Canada.* I understand that accepting the 2 free books and gifts places me under no obligation to buy anything. I can always return a shipment and cancel at any time. Even if I never buy another book, the two free books and gifts are mine to keep forever.

122/322 IDN FEG3

Name _____ (PLEASE PRINT) _____

Address _____ Apt. # _____

City _____ State/Prov. _____ Zip/Postal Code _____

Signature (if under 18, a parent or guardian must sign)

Mail to the **Reader Service:**
IN U.S.A.: P.O. Box 1867, Buffalo, NY 14240-1867
IN CANADA: P.O. Box 609, Fort Erie, Ontario L2A 5X3

Not valid to current subscribers to Love Inspired Larger-Print books.

**Are you a current subscriber to Love Inspired books
and want to receive the larger-print edition?
Call 1-800-873-8635 or visit www.ReaderService.com.**

* Terms and prices subject to change without notice. Prices do not include applicable taxes. Sales tax applicable in N.Y. Canadian residents will be charged applicable taxes. Offer not valid in Quebec. This offer is limited to one order per household. All orders subject to credit approval. Credit or debit balances in a customer's account(s) may be offset by any other outstanding balance owed by or to the customer. Please allow 4 to 6 weeks for delivery. Offer available while quantities last.

Your Privacy—The Reader Service is committed to protecting your privacy. Our Privacy Policy is available online at www.ReaderService.com or upon request from the Reader Service.

We make a portion of our mailing list available to reputable third parties that offer products we believe may interest you. If you prefer that we not exchange your name with third parties, or if you wish to clarify or modify your communication preferences, please visit us at www.ReaderService.com/consumerschoice or write to us at Reader Service Preference Service, P.O. Box 9062, Buffalo, NY 14269. Include your complete name and address.

LILP11B